The Urbana Free Library

To renew: call **217-367-4057**
or go to **urbanafreelibrary.org**
and select **My Account**

ALL MY GOODBYES

ALL MY GOODBYES

Mariana Dimópulos

Translated from the Spanish by
Alice Whitmore

TRANSIT
BOOKS

Published by Transit Books
2301 Telegraph Avenue, Oakland, California 94612
www.transitbooks.org

First published in Argentina under the title *Cada despedida*
by Adriana Hidalgo editora 2010

First published in English in Australia
by Giramondo Publishing 2017

FIRST US EDITION 2019

LIBRARY OF CONGRESS CONTROL NUMBER
2018961923

DESIGN & TYPESETTING
Justin Carder

DISTRIBUTED BY
Consortium Book Sales & Distribution
(800) 283-3572 | cbsd.com

Printed in the United States of America

9 8 7 6 5 4 3 2 1

This work was published within the framework of "Sur" Translation Support
Program of the Ministry of Foreign Affairs and Worship of the Argentine Repub-
lic. Obra editada en el marco del Programa "Sur" de Apoyo a las Traducciones
del Ministerio de Relaciones Exteriores y Culto de la República Argentina.

ALL MY GOODBYES

For Ariel, the only place

When I have occasionally set myself to consider the different distractions of men, the pains and perils to which they expose themselves at court or in war, whence arise so many quarrels, passions, bold and often terrible ventures, I have discovered that all the unhappiness of men arises from one single fact: that they cannot stay quietly in their own chamber.

—PASCAL

IT'S THE SAME THING TIME AND TIME AGAIN, shamelessly, tirelessly. It doesn't matter whether it's morning or night, winter or summer. Whether the house feels like home, whether somebody comes to the door to let me in. I arrive, and I want to stay, and then I leave.

In the early days, when we'd only just met and would wave hello to each other from afar, and sit down at the same table to drink our coffees, feigning indifference, Alexander liked to make fun of my nomadic ways. He would spend whole afternoons gently teasing me. It was amusing to him that I'd lived in three different houses during the short time I'd been in Heidelberg, and four different cities within the space of a year. I looked splendid, he told me, for someone so restless. Alexander spoke a slow Spanish, which sounded like velvet. But I was not splendid, and I never had been.

In our Berlin house, when we would stay up late talking, listening to Kolya breathing in his infant slumber, even Julia found it hard to believe that I'd been through eleven different jobs, not counting the one in the café where we'd met. "You were a baker,

11

an elevator operator? In a country with so few elevators . . ." she'd tease.

Like a pair of lovers we'd squander those hours of intimacy robbed from dinnertime, from books or television, since neither of us could be bothered to cook if Kolya had already eaten. Standing in the kitchen we'd nibble on a piece of bread or fruit and she would talk or ask me questions, wiping the benchtop a little, urging, insisting that there must be a reason for it. After a minute's silence she'd nudge me again, until finally I yielded her favorite sentence.

"Let's go to bed, I hate introspection."

We'd agree never to squander the hours like that again, and resolve to go to bed earlier next time. "A baker, and what else?" she'd pester with a smile, and I'd repeat the usual song: shelf-stacker, spare-parts sorter, patisserie attendant, green-grocer, waitress . . . grudgingly, I'd sigh out every stop on my professional pilgrimage. "Is that all?" Julia would mock. Then we'd stand there talking about her patients, about their diseases and ailments, until our knees and feet hurt. "One day you'll grow tired of moving around so much," she'd tell me. But she was wrong. It wasn't about growing tired, it was about *arriving*.

After all my travels, all those years lost and won and lost again; after testing a thousand times the raw stock of my being, which never seemed to cook; when at last I had found a man and I had loved him, they called me up so I could see how the story ended: the living room covered in blood from wall to wall, the ransacked house, the abandoned axe. What was I supposed to say? I extracted a tear from my eye and handed it to them, but they didn't want it. They wanted serious words and explanations. I stated that I had loved him and that I had met him a year before. That I didn't kill him. All of this was true.

It's easy to say it now: if only I'd never left, if only I'd never come back. When at the age of twenty-three I told my father I was going away to travel, he was seventy and had already relinquished a lot of things, but I wasn't one of them. He told me not to do it, not to leave him alone, that I would regret it. Hadn't I said I wanted to be a biologist, a wife, a mother? I replied that, yes, probably I had. But at twenty-three I was already ancient. I had regarded myself as incapable of sleeping in a bed, sitting in a chair, inhabiting a room, for too long.

"No problem," Alexander said, sipping at the coffee in his white cup. "When you go to lift the suitcase and realize it makes no sense, you just put it back down, unpack the clothes and hang them up in the wardrobe again. Then you find a piece of paper and you write down all the reasons why you shouldn't leave. You read over it two, three, four times. You learn it by heart. And that's it. You don't go." But when the time came I was never able to name a single reason for staying in that house or in that city, the place that was the cause of so much pain in my head, my stomach, my eyes during the insomnia of the night, and my shoes during the day.

Was I looking for a reason to stay in Heidelberg?

"Like me, for example," Alexander said.

And in the beginning I had also thought it possible. I'd imagined that he could be reason enough, imagined our shared home, our complicity beneath the sheets when, in silent agreement, we avoided love at all costs. Germany, for me, was

becoming something of a final destination, and for this reason all of those uncertainties were necessary. Those imaginings
cost me nothing. And sometimes I delighted in them secretly,
like a stowaway, knowing full well they would never become a
reality.

It's true that I left my father in the care of my older brothers,
that I sometimes visited him but not very often—not fully, and
not when he needed me. But my brothers had families and
important obligations to hide behind, whereas I, if I wanted
to avoid caring for my father, and if they asked me, could
only ever say no, no I can't, I can't, I'm going away. And so I
packed my suitcases and, armed with a sum of money that was
enough but by no means a fortune, I bought a ticket, and within twenty-four hours I was boarding a plane at Ezeiza airport.

"When will you be back?"

"Soon."

Our goodbyes were a non-event—it's a good thing men
don't cry. More than sad, my father was angry the last time I
saw him. When I arrived, I did what young people do when
they're in Madrid and they're Latin American and they haven't
crossed the oceans with the purpose of feeding a family back
home: I played for a while at the artist's life, I smoked hash-
ish, wore a scarf in my hair and worried, ostensibly, about the
grim fate of the world. The first house I lived in I shared with a
Uruguayan guy who played guitar and consumed himself with
boredom and melancholy. Because we were artists (of course),
someone recorded things with a camera, another improvised
musical laments in solidarity with the aforementioned grim

fate of the world; we painted the walls of the house in different colors, strung up amulets and other preposterous knick-knacks to lend the place atmosphere; we made a movie that promised to transform its impromptu director into a golden child of Latin American underground cinema, which, as things stood, was forced to subsist on the crumbs of compassion scattered by its European contemporaries. But all this I understood only much later. At the time all I understood was that, as the means to a cinematographic end, my bedroom was painted dark red, a fact that soon became unacceptable to me—the walls began to collapse above my shoulders, the window was too strict and diminutive, corralled in the corner: how could there be a window there? I asked myself. How had anyone ever been able to live in the presence of such a window? The days began to stretch to terrible lengths. The kitchen had always been a poky little place that nobody cleaned, except superficially, with a rank old cloth, as though out of guilt. But suddenly the shelf was inconceivable to me. And the bathroom? And the dining-room chairs? The kitchen shelf was just a thick groove in the wall. It had been wise not to get emotionally involved with either of my two housemates. I decided to do what I knew best.

My freedom always implies the slavery of another. So, my heart asks (and at heart I'm no good): if I enslave myself, does that mean someone else is set free?

The afternoon of the interrogation I found myself sitting opposite a fat man with a crew cut, who didn't know what to do with his hands when he spoke about blood. A strong wind had started up, and the vaulted roof of Madame Cupin's house seemed full of ghosts.

"You'd known them for how long?"

"Since last year. I arrived in November."

"And you've lived here on the farm since that time?"

"That's right."

They seemed like unnecessary questions. Did I know of any enemies? Had I overheard any threats, witnessed any arguments? Another man arrived and asked if he could have some water from the fridge. Despite the late hour, the heat of the day persisted. Suddenly, from one moment to the next, it seemed wrong to be sitting there at Madam Cupin's dining table. I stood up and got a chair from the kitchen, which I dragged over loudly under the watchful gaze of the policemen. And last night, what had happened?

"He told me I should spend the night in El Bolsón."

"Why?"

"Because of the insects."

The existence of those insects was to be proven shortly afterward, that same evening, although I'm not convinced their presence was enough to render my story plausible. Some caramel-colored bugs fell from the lamp, wandered slowly to the edge of the table, then continued on their way toward the Persian rug covering the floor. Some were just ordinary termites, others were bedecked with long translucent wings.

Didn't it strike me as suspicious that, on this precise night, he'd told me to sleep elsewhere, on account of a few bugs? No, what happened was a horrible coincidence. Were they supposed to believe me? they asked. Was I sure I hadn't left the house of my own accord? Or in collusion with someone else?

No: it was Marco, and no one else, who had ordered me to go into town the night before, leaving them alone, him and his mother, here at the Del Monje farm, on the side of the mountain, and the next day I found the two of them in my house, the door wide open, his arm covered with blood. I ran to look for help. What more did they want from me? I spilled more tears, sweet and salty. The axe belonged to Marco. They brought it to me and I identified it.

In Málaga I called myself Luisa; in Barcelona, Lola.

I'd lived in Heidelberg since autumn. I'd already fulfilled all the requirements imposed on recent arrivals to the city. I was a student, I had a room, medical insurance, a residency card. I was sealed and approved. In the employment agency on campus I read an advertisement for a job at the bakery at the foot of the castle. Since speaking on the telephone was impossible, I turned up at the bakery that same afternoon. I had the name of the person I was to speak to on a piece of paper in my jacket pocket, and one or two white lies prepared for good measure. The owner, who was married to the baker, had short hair and wore dark lipstick. Holding a child in her arms she ushered me into the patisserie, where we sat down and I accepted her offer of something to drink: just water. With great effort we commenced something resembling a conversation. She was used to working with foreigners, so long as they were students and understood the importance of being punctual, she hastened to explain. The job was simple—how hard could it be to wrap up loaves of bread, pass them over the counter, accept and return euros? But everything had to be done expeditiously, without an instant's hesitation. Were we agreed? We were. At six o'clock the next morning, long before sunrise, I walked around the bakery taking notes in my gibberish script, tortuously inscribed on a loose leaf of paper. I noted down the names of all the different breads and German pastries as she dictated them to me, pointing at each compartment behind the glass counter. Good morning, good morning. A man came in. Two loaves of bread. Two *what*? Two loaves of bread, he'd ordered. What else.

The baker's assistant would emerge every now and then bearing trays hot from the oven, and it was difficult not to burn myself as I transferred the bread rolls to the baskets, just as it was difficult, under the half-compassionate, half-inquisitive gaze of the owner, with the customers waiting there on the other side of the counter, to avoid letting a precious *brötchen* fall from my hands to the floor, where it would roll away, far from our feet. The owner told me she'd studied at the university, she'd wanted to be an orthodontist, she liked teeth, she even liked blood a little bit, and I struggled my way as best I could through the mud of our conversation while she arranged the cakes in the cake fridge. I received the cakes from the hands of the pastry chef who, strangely enough, was not fat, despite being affable. And her husband, the baker? He was always "out the back." The morning passed like a whirlwind, the kind which presages a downpour that never comes.

In the afternoon it was more of the same, and again the next day, with customers entering the bakery to spit their more or less inventive riddles at me: three croissants, a jar of jam. A *jar*? What on earth was a *jar*? When they left—which was almost never, for it seemed they only ever entered—I would take the opportunity to resume my battle with the German language, muttering words under my breath, repeating the vocabulary I'd learned, if I'd learned any, and thinking about my father, without wanting to think about him at all. He had always treated me as a distinct and determinate particle in the universe. Now, in the planetary system that was Heidelberg, everybody went about completing their individual elliptical orbits, glimmering in lazy rotations, and I was nothing more than a distant star, barely a reflection of the others' light. I also thought about doña Carmen, who so often had complained to me, insisting as we scrubbed with our four hands the patio of the hotel in La Mancha: "Speak slowly, my girl, that's quite an accent you've got there!" Now I wondered: if doña Carmen, who spoke my language, had complained about my accent, how would new acquaintances react to my labored attempts at German?

We're just testing out physical states, my father always used to say. Even stones. Precambrian stones are fundamentally no different from the wings of a fly. He had that air of self-sufficient competence that doctors and naturalists have. The harmony of the stone breaks down into baryons just as a housefly does. It simply holds its form for a longer period of time, et cetera, et cetera. When I left Buenos Aires at twenty-three I had long been tired of listening to him, even though I loved him biblically, perhaps even more than that.

I'd been a foreigner for barely a month. After the artists' share house I spent a week in a first-floor apartment in the center of Madrid, and didn't pine at all for my old housemates, nor for the red room I'd left behind. My new bedroom was old, constantly invaded by the sounds of music, shouting, and the loud opinions of the people eating in the tapas bar below. Although I thought about it more than once, I never quite managed to drag myself out of bed, stuff myself into a pair of jeans and join them downstairs, to put a drink in my belly and gaze at their chests or their eyes. Instead I remained in bed, listening to their repetitive conversations. There was no end to their stupidity and their happiness. Stale smoke sifted into my bedroom. Each night lasted a thousand nights. Soon I had motive enough; a week after moving in I packed up my possessions, which were scant, and went to the bus station. I'd been told about a town called Almagro; Almagro was very pretty, or so people said, and although I wasn't entirely sure I was looking for somewhere pretty, or beautiful, or lovely, I got on the bus and a few hours later I was there.

"Tourist?" they asked me.

I don't know if it was the situation that made me a liar, but as I've said before, I don't have a good heart. I replied that yes, I was, and for a period of time that seemed like too long I became a tourist. I fulfilled all my obligations, visited places, marveled at them. The plaza, the old theater, the motionless people behind the arched porticos. You have to go to Spain to understand porticos. That civilian zoo, that arid stage; and then, suddenly, everything became what it should have been, and I no longer marveled at it. My dalliance with the century-old aberration of tourism was over. I selected a hotel with a patio and a medieval cistern, and met doña Carmen. I lied to her, too. What else could I have done? It's not that I was trying to forget something, to undo a terrible past, to abandon someone or destroy myself; it's simply that I was finally old enough now, and although I'd tried many times back home in Buenos Aires, I'd never managed to come to terms with my own mean spirit. I spent the first few weeks in one of the hotel's most isolated rooms, at my own request. I did nothing but read and watch television. When doña Carmen came out to hose down the patio I would study her through the window, especially her arms and her waist, her predictably floral dresses, her high-heeled shoes. She was a beautiful woman, in her way. She tackled her chores with tremendous energy and asked nothing of anyone, except her two sons, who lived far away. She didn't even need a man, or so I gathered from her comments one evening when, on account of the heat, she threw herself on the sofa in the foyer, cheeks burning. For me, *nada*, she said; nothing, my girl, just a bit of bread, a slice of jamón, and a cold beer. She was neat, tidy, she knew what it meant to sweat. One time I went out to the patio and started to help her with the cleaning, which, despite the argument we struck up, she eventually allowed. In the delicatessen down by the theater I overheard a man say that doña Carmen had once been a whore. He didn't say it in a disapproving tone, he might even have been an ex-client, unless of course doña Carmen had practiced her profession in some other part of Spain.

That doña Carmen had once been a whore, in Almagro or in any other town, is a lie.

Sitting in the university café in Heidelberg, opposite the main square, Alexander asked me why I'd worked in the bakery at the foot of the castle, and then as a glass-stacker in IKEA, and why indeed I was currently employed as an auto-parts sorter at the ABB factory, if *in reality* I was a biologist. Imagine traveling forty kilometers by bus every day! He said he could organize for me to give Spanish lessons, maybe help me find a scholarship, even get me a job at the chemical testing lab on campus. All of these things he said, stroking my knee under the table without looking at me, as though the movement were purely coincidental.

What do I believe in, after all this? I believe in Alexander, in Kolya, in Julia. In a Turkish warrior. And I believe in *him*, of course. In the fact that I left home at twenty-three and returned ten years later, finally to fall in love with a man. I believe in those pilgrim years, when staying put was not an option, those years spent in a kind of conspiracy with habit and daily routine, despite myself, but always with a ticket under my arm, or perhaps up my dirty sleeve, always with a passage to somewhere else at the ready. I would always arrive with the intention of staying. And even then I wouldn't stay. I don't understand what the word *for* is for. Being useful is of no use to me.

Athens airport has a great big staircase where the wind, Greek and dry, burns my face.

In Heidelberg, Alexander tells me again about the campus laboratory just outside the city. I feign surprise, then reply that I am sulfur intolerant. But the idea was not new to me at all.

"What about the laboratory?" one of my brothers asked me in Buenos Aires, when I told him I was leaving.
    "Where are you going?"

"Away."

For some time they'd been planning to set up a clinical analysis and bacteriology lab in which my participation, they believed, was imperative. The project had been my father's idea, obviously. It was his way of exorcising old age. They all practiced with zeal the alchemy of daily life: the kids, the wife, the job. Their dosages were always wrong, almost always badly timed. Maybe the laboratory, they told themselves.

"You're going for what," my father had said without inflecting the question.

I began with the practical reasons and followed up with the personal ones. I presented a solid defense: the possibility of finding a job in the sciences (although I didn't want to), of pursuing further study (although I didn't plan on studying either). I said nothing about saving money; he would never have believed me. What more could I do? I was young, I had concocted a few firm convictions. After my somewhat heated oration I fell silent.

"You won't be happy over there either," my father decreed.

He told me about his travels in China when my mother was still alive and I still wasn't born, twenty-five, thirty years ago. His victory over me was frugal, half-smiling, like everything else about him.

Exhausted by a long day at work, I fall asleep. But the travel bug never rests, and it lays traps for me day and night.

One morning, at a little hotel in the Spanish town called Almagro, doña Carmen grew tired of me. A month and a half had passed since I'd left Buenos Aires, and I still thought I was on holiday.

"Think about it, my girl: the sun, the beach!"

She had a sister in Málaga, on the coast. At this time of year I could get a good deal on accommodations. I went, knowing full well that three weeks in doña Carmen's hotel had not been long enough for the furniture, the old television set, to render themselves unfathomable to me. Given a little more time (it was all about *time*) things would have ended the way they so often did, in later years. The arrival—from dinner, say, or from the supermarket. The setting of the handbag on the floor. The glance around the room. What is that chest of drawers, that bed? What is that rug (if there was a rug)? What are those curtains? Suddenly the chair is archaic, there is no use for it. The bedroom is abandoned, the bathroom and its mirrors incomprehensible. How can it be abandoned, I wonder, if until so recently it was my very own room? How, if that blanket is mine, the towels freshly replaced just this morning? And yet, it has all become unfathomable to me. Did I really think I'd been living within these four walls this whole time? It was just an illusion. A lackluster magic trick, utterly profane. I exit the room, then walk back into it. What happens? The same thing: the ludicrous furniture, the mute door. I'm a fool, I tell myself, and I sit down. Perhaps I look out the window. I see the same old landscape. How did I get up every morning and look out that window at the same old landscape? That isn't life, I tell myself, there must be something more.

"And the neighbor up the hill? They had a fight over a water channel. Do you know anything about that? Did you ever hear anything about a death threat?"

The policeman spat when he spoke. Meanwhile, I heard the ghosts of the wind circling in the vaulted roof of Madame Cupin's house.

"Once he came over on a horse and trampled the marigolds. But I never heard anything about a death threat."

"Do you still assert that you left the house that night because of the bugs?"

"I do."

When I wake up I make a long calculation, with functions and algorithms. It happens every morning, and the result is always me. This is surprising.

I bade farewell to doña Carmen with the promise that I would pass through Almagro again on my way back to Madrid. I knew I wouldn't, but I would have liked to in some other future that wasn't my own. When I said goodbye and embraced her thick body, warmed by the La Mancha sun, I understood that it would be the last time. She no longer mattered to me. With that same embrace, doña Carmen had dissolved into nothing. Yes, I would stay with her sister. We'd see each other again soon, soon. I was hardly paying attention. I went to Málaga without closing my eyes once, taking in every centimeter of the passing landscape. That same day I managed to find doña Carmen's sister's guesthouse. I examined the front porch and decided it was impossible; I wandered a few blocks to the right and another few to the left, as though I knew where I was headed, and on a corner I would certainly have described as dull I found another hotel. It had two stars; this seemed like a lot.

I spent two days coming and going at the appropriate times, towel tucked beneath my arm. Upon arriving at my destination I would half-unfold it and search for a patch of shade. But that would never work, not in a place like this. Those who believed otherwise were profoundly mistaken. It was impossible to remain in Málaga, let alone *live* in Málaga. To be in Málaga was to be mistaken down to one's bones—gravely, feverishly mistaken. I would sit down as best I could at the beach, without fully unfolding my towel, as I've already mentioned, in a patch of shade if I could find one, and keenly study the improbability of everything. Those umbrellas? Absolutely not. That coast? It was impossible to remain seated; if I stood up, it took everything I had not to break into a run. But where would I go? The Mediterranean, that ancient sea, was a dumb song.

I got to my feet and went to the water. There was a ball floating on the waves and two boys running back and forth along the sand, neither daring to go in and retrieve it. They watched spellbound as the tide drew it in and out.

They asked me for help and I told them there was no way I was going into the sea to rescue their horrible ball.

That last bit is a lie. Nobody ever asked me anything.

"Any family members you know of?"

"One brother. He lives in Chile. He's an architect."

"And what is your opinion of him?"

"No opinion. He's tall. He writes poems in a little book."

Shortly afterward, the next day in fact, I met Stefan. I had gone to the beach and was forced to sit on the sand to get some

sun. I saw him from afar, walking with a certain nonchalance.
A dog was following him. I later discovered that the dog wasn't
his, although he walked as if it belonged to him, shoulders
pressed forward, back heavy, exuding that radiant resignation
particular to men walking with their dogs. They passed a few
meters from me and stopped a little further along. There was
a red car. Stefan seemed to be arguing with someone inside,
someone hidden by the reflection coloring the windscreen. At
the risk of humiliating myself in front of both him and his dog,
I stood up as if to walk over and alert them to my presence.
My sudden stroke of curiosity was ridiculous, but still I continued all the way to the asphalt. I glanced emphatically at them
again, but they didn't even turn around, nor did I walk over
to meet them. Instead I deliberately crossed to the other side
of the street. All I could think was that I was wrong: wrong to
leave, wrong to stay. Because my head was so vacant I thought
about things a lot, applying a degree of patience and detail that
stirred no pride in me. So I ended up at Málaga train station
and bought a ticket back to Madrid. From there, I thought, I
would return to Buenos Aires and put an end to this farcical
vacation. I had left for the sake of leaving, nothing more. And
it was the same thing now, I told myself as I paid for the ticket:
I hoped Madrid would soon become untenable, boring in her
brilliance, with that brilliant boredom only cities can evoke. It
was enough to detest the people there mildly, so long as I had
nothing: if there were ties, I would untie them; if there were
agreements, I would disclaim them. Then would come the triumphant moment, when the suitcases are packed and I haul
them onto the final carriage, close the final door.

The entire expedition out of Buenos Aires would be

rendered inoffensive, a round-the-world trip in Hispanic miniature. And my father would have his small victory, seeing me back home, and I would happily let him have it, because he was old and that was a secret neither of us dared to reveal. But that's not how it happened. That same night, with my suitcases packed and my hotel bill settled, I saw Stefan again. This time, instead of a dog, he was accompanied by a little boy. He came into the bar where I was eating dinner, took a look around and selected a table outside. I tried not to insist, with my eyes or with my thoughts, concentrating instead on the fish I had just been served and on the usual inane reflections of the traveler, such as the cost of the next day's travels, where I was going to sleep in Madrid, whether there was still a metro ticket floating around in one of my pockets. I was trying to distract myself, because he was in Málaga and I, to all intents and purposes, had already left Málaga. The meal tasted of nothing in particular; I finished it without any real satisfaction, mistakenly believing that I might as well have eaten nothing at all. The amenities, the furnishings, the paintings inside the bar all seemed offensive to me, nothing less than a slap in the face. Even the waiters, the other diners, they were all wrong, every leg, every hoisting of fork to mouth was wrong.

"Where's the dog?" I asked him.

Stefan lifted his gaze from his plate and hesitated for a moment, sizing me up. It took him only a second to approve of my attire and frame. He smiled splendidly, clearly pleased.

"The dog from today? You're right, there was a dog following me around all day, but it's not mine. Is it yours?"

"No."

"Please, sit down. This is my son Andrei. Do you like children?"

He stretched out the word *children*. I didn't reply.

He offered me something to drink and we were more than friendly with one another, there behind our wine glasses. First we had the obligatory conversation about Málaga, our respective places of origin, whether seaside or mountains, both of us making subtle signs, never letting our sentences stray too close to intimacy. That's what the night was for. With the excuse of stretching our legs we set off for a stroll. The little boy, who was walking between us, insisted on grabbing my skirt and flicking it. I didn't find this amusing. After a while we stopped to look at the sky and the stars. Because the little boy loved to look at the sky, according to Stefan. But the kid thought he'd seen a lizard and started to run around in circles, repeating the same two or three words like a sad little bird. His father paid scant attention to him, casting the occasional monosyllable in his direction, random words of approval, until the kid whirled away again beyond the shrubs. When he circled back past us he pointed at me.

"Are you cold?" he asked.

Stefan was standing behind me now, with his arms around me. I replied, with strange solemnity, that I was. When the kid left again, Stefan began to murmur the names of the stars he knew. I told him which ones I preferred, this one, that one, as if discussing products on a supermarket shelf, pretending I'd never until that moment examined the sky the astronomers had invented. It was cheap romanticism, by anyone's standards. We both knew that. The monotonous melody of myself traced slow circles in my head. I think I might have lied a little, passing myself off as a young doña Carmen. The kid came past one last time and clung to his father's trousers, said he missed his mama.

"It's late," Stefan said, and loosened his embrace.

I accompanied them to the hotel at a brisk pace, and bid them farewell at the door without so much as a kiss, thinking about how I would never see either of them again. I abhorred the thought of my body touching the bed, I would have done anything to fall asleep on my feet. Turns out I was wrong about never seeing them again.

As if from a tall staircase, I fell into introspection.

I leave because I cannot stay, or I leave *so that* I cannot stay. The kind of quandary Alexander would have delighted in, chatting there in the café, seated with or without our hands entwined under the table, having granted each other a night of sex the evening before. I don't believe it, I'm certain of it: he was in love with me from the very beginning. He wasn't joking when he told me to stay—at least until the following year, when he'd have finished his degree, so we could make plans together, either there in Heidelberg or in some other corner of the globe. Alexander was German but not overly so, he wasn't tremendously German or European, and yet he had that cheerful way of preparing for the future because he believed it belonged to him, although it's also true that he was constantly and tactlessly suspicious of his own freedom.

I try cheerfulness. Then I lie.

"Don't stay here on your own. Go and sleep in town," the policemen recommended that night. The fat one with the crew cut offered me one of his thick hands to shake when he left. But I didn't listen to them. I decided to stay in Madame Cupin's house full of ghosts. Once I was alone the sadness engulfed me. I couldn't even eat a bowl of soup or a piece of bread. Lying down to sleep on the canopy bed felt like sacrilege, but I did it anyway, trying not to think about what had just happened here at the Del Monje farm. The pill the neighbors had given me began to take effect around midnight, and when I closed my eyes I felt them falling from the roof, down toward the bed, onto my face and legs, felt them crawling between the sheets: the little caramel-colored insects Marco had promised.

Sometimes Alexander would go away to "think a little."

"Think about what?" I'd ask. He would just stroke my hand in reply, finding no amusing words to embellish his withdrawal. I wouldn't see him for several days. We had our rituals: in the city of Heidelberg there was a number of specified places where we would meet and pretend to be surprised. He was going away, he told me, to think. About what? I wondered. I confused his withdrawal with introspection, and other emotional trinkets like doubt and sentimentality. I told him I'd rather classify spare auto parts and package ball bearings, or bread, into boxes and crates, than sit in front of some German or Swiss mountain to "think." When he returned, neither the same nor renewed, he never told me where he'd been. And to me this seemed like a mystery from another world—the fact that someone could leave their home and come back to that same home a few days later, back to the same café packed with haggard students to drink the same coffee, with me. On those afternoons I'd talk to him about everything: my father, the laboratory we didn't build together, my time in Madrid with the artists, doña Carmen, each and every whim that had led me to the place I was in now. I think I changed Stefan's name, in case they knew each other. I don't just believe it, I'm certain of it. I remember, I know. What else is there?

I told doña Carmen about my father and the family laboratory while we scoured (as she used to put it) the patio of the Almagro hotel. Then I told Alexander, in Heidelberg, about my father and doña Carmen, and about Stefan in Málaga, while we drank watery coffee at the university. I told Julia, in Berlin, about my odd jobs and love affairs as we stood around in the kitchen not eating dinner, nibbling on bread like a pair of sleepy birds, leaning first on one leg then the other. But with Marco, ten years later, when I returned to Argentina and spent a year on the Del Monje farm, I never spoke of any of this, and he never asked. There was no need—perhaps because the intimation of love between us was sufficient.

It was late. We didn't even attempt to lower the canoe into the water. There was too much wind and too little sun. We watched the way the light swept the far side of the lake, flowing toward the peak of the mountain, until all it touched were the gases of an especially clear and benevolent atmosphere. I rested my head against the grass and thought I could hear the sound of the Earth moving, slowly turning its back on the day. But Marco had sat down close by, and the certainty of his presence engulfed me.

"The sun's gone down," I said, in a comfortably childlike way.

But I didn't dare touch him.

"Yes. We should make a fire. I'll find some branches."

Soon it began to smell of night, and Marco still hadn't returned from his expedition into the woods surrounding the lake. The wind had dropped but it was too late to cross to the other shore—rowing in the dark would have been pointless and dangerous. An orchestra of crickets was playing nearby, and somewhere a dog barked impatiently. Nature was black and blue. Nowhere did I sense its atoms or covalent bonds; even the woods behind me seemed to have stopped exhaling carbon monoxide. Everything was paused. I rested my head on the grass and closed my eyes, trying to listen. I could no longer hear the Earth's revolutions. I couldn't even hear my own heartbeat.

Marco returned when it was very dark, and told me he hadn't found anything to eat. He made a nice fire and we warmed our hands.

Why, or to what end? Sometimes I don't know.

In the Heidelberg bakery, if by some miracle a few minutes passed without any customers walking in, without the owner wandering out the front to check the state of the glass cabinet or behind the counter to check the state of the floor and the breadbaskets, I enjoyed looking out at the cobblestone walkway of the Hauptstraße, when it was empty and also when it was full of Japanese tourists, for example, on their way to the castle. In the three years I lived in Heidelberg I never went up to the castle, nor did I feel the need to: it was something I neither promised myself nor prohibited. Such things simply didn't interest me, in spite of Alexander's surprise, or perhaps because of it. But my curiosity knew no bounds when it came to watching the Hauptstraße, peering through the latticework of pretend cakes and decorations piled up in the shop window. These were precious minutes of innocuous daydreaming, during which I was safe from the treacherous mud of my own thoughts. I'd watch the Japanese tourists pass by in their invisible shoes, armed with their miniature cameras, imagining that they made no noise as they stepped over the cobblestones. I would happily suspend myself in that simple activity, thinking about the castle, about whether they'd like it, about what images they'd bring back in their cameras. It was a pleasant pastime. But, slowly, the empty lot of my head filled back up with volatile and unstable things, like methane gas. This is how it works: a pact is made, between ourselves and the world at large, and we step out of it onto the wicked path of introspection.

In IKEA, too, when I was working as, or, if you like, when I *was* a shelf-stacker in the dining and kitchen area, I would sometimes snatch a moment to hunt for something, something I could lose myself in mentally, taking care not to drift too far toward melancholy, or the sleek fear that always accompanies stolen fantasies. But such moments were rare. More often than not the monotonous music they poured over our heads from four o'clock in the morning, when my shift started, spared us from the perils of meditation. It was such terribly nice, insipid, sycophantic music. Specifically chosen to accompany the shoppers who, at their own placid pace, would wander at length through the store, picking up an object here, another there, until they arrived as if by magic at the checkout and, barely conscious by this point, pay whatever amount the cash register dictated. In the palace of IKEA everything was swathed in color. But in us—or in *me*, at least—the lights and music had the opposite effect. They always had, ever since that first early morning when I'd entered the enormous complex by the back door to receive my yellow polo shirt with the logo on it, the one my coworkers were so proud of, and my blue pants. I was taken to the warehouse, where I was received by the assistant to the stock manager who, perched on a forklift, gave me instructions as I followed him up and down the looming aisles of shelves with their thousands of boxes, stepping in time with the rhythm of his machine so that he didn't have to waste a single second on me. He seemed to have a taste for authority. Breakfast would be served at eight, he said proudly, and at five-thirty we'd get a ten-minute coffee and cigarette break. When I walked into the store, my female colleagues (who apparently didn't care to mingle with their male counterparts and seemed for all the world like some kind of secret cult) showed me the shelves lined with cups and glasses. I was to devote myself to those shelves until breakfast. How was it possible that I hadn't finished yet, they asked me when, silently, they stood up and abandoned the boxes that until a moment ago they'd been so immersed in; how was it possible that I hadn't managed to finish the shelves? The boss was coming after breakfast to give things a once over. Which boss? My boss, and their boss, they grumbled. She was coming after breakfast and she'd hit the roof when she saw that the shelves of glasses and teacups were unfinished. And what about this broken plate? Despite my desire to communicate, I was incapable of explaining myself or asking for details. My tongue languished like a long worm at the back of my throat, neither able nor willing to articulate, comfortable in its placid barbarism.

Arriving in Berlin turned out to be much easier than a lot of the other things I'd done. When I arrived in Berlin it felt like, for the first time, I'd done something right. I explored the city extensively, and right away I could tell that this was a place I could adopt, one that I could love in its entirety. I'm exaggerating, of course. But I enjoyed idealizing the people I saw in the streets, and I enjoyed the belief that, here among the apparent inequalities, the drunks, the drug dealers and their shabby clothes, there was something hidden, something buried like the old unexploded bombs from the war, some kind of magnet to which I might stick, like a noble metal. But we know from our hydrogen and our oxygen that we are water as well as dust. And water runs.

I got off the train at Tiergarten and spent my first night nearby. I paid a lot and slept little, and dedicated the next morning to trawling the web of subway tunnels in order to track down a student hotel more suited to my budget on the other side of the city. In Berlin, the idea of "the other side" was true—in Berlin you could cross over, you could be either here or there simply by traversing the old border. I took great pleasure in this. Later, Julia insisted that I was the only foreigner in all of Berlin who could trace the precise location of the wall that now, twenty years after its fall, still stretched like a fine electric fence between the East and the West of what were once two Germanys. At any point in the city, Julia said (and it was true), I could place my foot down in the correct spot and say: East, West. Or I could cross over to one side and say one thing and then cross over to the other side and believe the exact opposite.

"So you're staying then, here in Berlin?" Julia would ask me. And sometimes I'd say yes in the East and also in the West. But other times no, and since we lived a block from one of the many curving edges of the border, overlooking the greenish arm of the canal, I would suddenly go out into the rain, or into the snow, which was almost always dirty and insufficient, and cross over to the other side to think the opposite. This mostly happened in moments of outrage, when my room in Julia and Kolya's house seemed to compress suddenly into a tiny cube and I was forced to leave, regardless of what I had on—whether rugged up or not, whether in shoes or slippers—so that, if only for a few minutes, I could breathe once more the seemingly free air.

I waste a whole morning on a single sentence. It takes me precisely five hours to invent a German sentence.

"Where can I put glasses other side during the day that remains?"

The boss takes a whole minute to turn and look at me, an entire minute with her back to me, even though I know she's heard me.

She looks me up and down. It doesn't even qualify as disdain, the look she gives me.

"Work?" she answers. She lifts a finger and points to a box filled with red and green cushions. I lower my head. Off I go.

For Julia (who, unlike me, was good) it was sometimes difficult to understand. She would speak to me about my symptoms, about her patients, contemplating the point of a pencil with which she took notes at home. She would ask me questions in passing, weaving theories. I would seek revenge by locking myself in my bedroom for entire afternoons. Or at night, furtively, while they were sleeping, I'd steal to the kitchen and commit some random act of vandalism. But it wasn't like that during my first few months in Berlin, when I still hadn't met Julia and was working as a waitress, serving breakfasts in a Moabit hotel. One long and somehow bitter morning, gray and distant, a man who was drinking his coffee very early along with two other men in the hotel dining room asked me why I laughed when I served them the meager plate of provisions that passed for breakfast: two slices of bread, a slip of butter encased in plastic.

"Why are you laughing?" he asked me. He was wide. He didn't fit in the chair. He must have measured hundreds of meters in circumference.

"I'm not laughing, I'm smiling," I said.

Then the man sitting beside him wanted to know why I was smiling at them, if smiling wasn't a prerequisite for serving breakfast. Even though my tongue no longer dozed at the back of my throat like a dormouse in the winter, I didn't answer them. I had nothing to say. They had snatched away all my reasons. It was true: I had nothing to smile about, considering I started work at six in the morning, rain or shine, then tidied up the kitchen after breakfast and set to slicing vegetables for the restaurant, then in the tedious afternoons reordered all the disorder until my legs and feet were stiff and painful. From that morning on I tried to remain serious at all times, but whenever I approached a table, occupied for example by Chinese diners, or German ones, friendly or unfriendly, my lips inevitably contorted into the same smile, which might well have been a plea for help. I spent countless mornings and afternoons trying to wipe that sad, servile smile off my face. Countless days pulling down the corners of my mouth, in vain. I was renting a room from a retired couple in Neukölln, the walls and doors of which seemed to be constructed of painted cardboard, with nothing but an old oven to heat the place, and I got to work at six in the morning, rain or shine, and the whole time I had this stupid half-smile on my face, and I got on the subway and I got off the subway, suspecting the whole time that something was wrong, but I tried and I tried, and I had a thousand arguments for anyone who disbelieved the authenticity of my grimace and the sincerity of my two windows.

I rest my head on the grass and confirm that I can no longer hear the Earth moving, that, however impossibly, it seems to have stopped turning.

My father was still alive then; it had been two years since I'd moved to Berlin, and seven since I'd left Buenos Aires. Not too long ago we'd spoken on the phone, avoiding any major reproaches. He told me about his grandchildren, with no great degree of complicity—he presumed I wasn't interested in the charms of childhood. As a man of science he was wary of falling into sentimentalism, something he'd done very rarely over the course of his life, and nobody would dare accuse him of it, not I then nor anyone since. Between the silences and other trifles we hid our truths. He asked me where I was working, then laughed with tender sarcasm and repeated my answer: "potato and sausage vendor." He liked poking fun at me. "So you're a sausage peddler," he persisted, his naturalist's heart a little wounded—the same heart that had foreseen so much science in my future. And it was a relief to tell him that he was right and to accept, over the telephone, from seventeen thousand kilometers away, communicating by the grace of electromagnetic waves and orbiting satellites, that he held, and always would hold, the winning hand, that his litany on restlessness was like a salve to me because it was old and because I knew it by heart. At seventy-eight years of age, still a physicist and skeptic by trade, he told me not to persevere with my searching, he told me that the notion of space was as obsolete as that of ether. "Don't persevere because it doesn't make sense," because on no continent, on no planet, did there exist, strictly speaking, a position like the one we were habituated to; strictly speaking, nowhere existed anywhere. I didn't want to speak strictly. But what did I do? I agreed with him. From seventeen thousand kilometers away I set in motion an electromagnetic wave to tell him: yes.

But I didn't go home when he died. I went afterward, and only to witness the death of another. Having spent ten years in Europe, I only visited Buenos Aires for a few weeks before continuing south. I'd been on the brink of closing an erratic cycle, and refrained from doing so. The grid of the city descended over me like a net, and I began to think again about the street names and street numbers, about the interweaving lines of the subway and the exhalations of the buses. One of my brothers had picked me up from the airport and agreed to let me stay at his house, because ours—that is, my father's, mine and theirs—had been swiftly auctioned to discharge the family's debts. My brother explained this to me as he tried to placate one of his children, wailing tirelessly for a chocolate or a soda from the back seat of the car. It was nearly impossible to live in that suburban house of his, amid the scattered school supplies and the silence of the cleaning lady. Everyone suspected I was returning from some kind of failure, I could sense it in their condescending glances and the vagueness of their questions. All that seemed to matter to them, the one thing they reminded me about again and again, was that I hadn't been there for my father's funeral. One of my sisters-in-law pointed out that at least he hadn't suffered too much. "Not too much," she said. "Not excessively." They spoke about my father as though he were an expensive piece of furniture nobody wanted. I asked them if they'd spoken about him this way while he'd been alive, but they didn't understand the question well enough to be offended. Why bother fighting, since we were all so good and civil? That Sunday, one week after my return, leafing through the newspaper in the peaceful wake of the daily breakfast chaos, I found an advertisement for berry-picking jobs in the south. It said the harvesting season was about to start. I packed up my things that night, muttered an explanation that nobody seemed to pay any mind to, and made my way to the Retiro bus terminal. There were no buses leaving that night.

Are you sure? Not even with a different company? *Nada de nada*. The last buses only go as far as Santa Rosa. I slept across the road, in a traveler's hotel on Avenida Libertador. In the hotel I played at being a foreigner; I even pretended I couldn't understand the reception clerk's Spanish. Was I a bad actress? To me it felt like the height of authenticity, but my performance didn't ring true.

I could smell the night, heard the complaint of a frightened dog. But I wasn't afraid. The Earth had stopped turning on its axis. "Impossible!" my father would have said.

The harvest still hadn't started when I arrived at Las Golondrinas. At the volunteer fire station they assured me it would be more convenient or more affordable to stay in the town of El Bolsón, but ever since that first apartment in Madrid—the one I'd shared with the melancholy musician and the supposed filmmaker—I'd been wary of artists and artisans, and that's exactly what the name "El Bolsón" suggested to me. I bid farewell to the firefighters (there were three of them) and crossed Route 40, heading toward the lower slope of the mountain. At the first gully, just before the terrain began to rise, I found a little cabin, typically alpine, complete with ugly furniture, in which to spend the night. The owners said they were brothers. They soon confided that this place wasn't what it used to be, that now they had to turn the radio right up so they wouldn't hear the trucks on Route 40 rolling toward the Andes. They owned a complex of eight tiny units just like mine, surrounded on all sides by pine forest. I decided from the outset that I wouldn't share anything of myself with these bearded brothers, nor with any of my neighbors in the other cabins. Who were they? Families spending the first half of summer far from the city, couples enclosing themselves in wooden tents only to discover that they were as incapable of living together as they were of separating. Watching them come and go, I felt reassured; Las Golondrinas was not the kind of place where anything transcendental occurred, it was not the kind of place where ideas happened, or where one promised oneself anything true, or even probable, or even kind. I was wrong. It was a forest solely of pines, perfumed. In bed I dreamt of bonfires.

Strawberries were appearing in the nearby fields, but there were already several volunteers enlisted to harvest them. I was told to look for work higher up the mountain. I left that same afternoon. There was a cattle fence, and two tracks imprinted in the grass where I entered. Farther along three houses appeared, two very close to one another, the third set apart a little. There was a walnut tree bent over the patio, and beneath it a sheep with a black muzzle, tethered and bleating. I stopped and applauded. Then he appeared.

Rest is a form of movement, he insisted. My father liked axioms, he was always contradicting things. Me? I was so irritated by his puzzles. To such an extent that, sometimes, when I was bringing a cup of tea over to the desk where he worked, I would accidentally spill it all over myself. Sitting there at his desk he would talk about movement and I would scurry along, slowly burning my fingers.

"How can you do this to us?" Julia screamed. It was the first time I ever saw her angry.

But years later, in Berlin, I'd learned how to keep my pulse steady. At work in the mediocre hotel, with my half-smile, and especially in the café in the city center, where I served the hottest and fullest cups without spilling a single drop. Until then I'd been through several different jobs, known and inhabited seven, eight, nine different bedrooms, and in each one I'd fantasize about overstaying my welcome, because I still didn't know myself well enough, I still wasn't convinced about who I was. Rather than fall into introspection and rummage around in my own muddy depths I preferred to pack my bags, to inaugurate something, the *next thing*. In the Berlin patisserie, on Friedrichstraße, I met Julia. She was on one side of the counter and I was on the other. I began to recognize her on her second or third visit. Sometimes she would come with Kolya and sit him down on one of the high bar stools, causing quite a scandal among the clientele, who murmured their displeasure the way one murmurs one's displeasure in places like Berlin: with their eyes, without a word. Kolya had a yellow head of hair that always recalled summer, and round Russian eyes that, no matter what the circumstances, always made you want to weep. Julia was interested in me; she would come to the café and sit close to the coffee machine where I produced the espressos and macchiatos. I noticed a certain clinical curiosity mixed with her general affection for me, which often led her to interrogate me, casually, while Kolya sat eating happily, burying his nose in bread and butter. And although it was never easy for us to maintain a conversation due to the constant interruptions of other customers, which meant we had to keep repeating ourselves clumsily to make the most of our brief opportunities, I discovered that she was a trauma therapist, that she had separated from Kolya's father not long ago, that she believed in the soul, in the psyche, in the afterlife, believed acutely in the humanity of mankind. She spouted grand ideas, and in her mouth the ideas were beautiful. Later on, when I lived with her in the ground floor apartment that gave onto the canal and the old Wall, nestled between Treptow and Kreuzberg, she told me she was proud of her beliefs, and of the patient, earnest naivety with which she approached her clinical cases, mine included. She marveled at the fact that, *over there* (as she referred to my old life in Buenos Aires) I'd studied biology, then chemistry—first organic, then inorganic. What could possibly be so fascinating about chlorides? For her, believer in dreams and the subconscious, octahedral silicates were insignificant. Who knows, maybe she fell in love with me too. One night, standing in the kitchen of the apartment, picking at our bread and fruit like insects while Kolya slept in the adjoining room, she told me confusedly that yes, she did love me; she invited me to cross the meter-wide divide that separated us and let her hold me. But my tears, or my laughter, did not come from a need for affection or consolation. I found it neither scandalous nor soothing that Julia thought she desired me that night, because we were alone and we loved each other, and Berlin would have been the best possible place for such a love. Did I mistrust her? No, I could never have mistrusted her. But I didn't cross the kitchen and go to her, nor did I change the subject. Julia remained where she was, leaning against the kitchen counter, and asked me, as always, to repeat my long list of odd jobs and occupations, because she liked to listen to me, because she thought of my misery as something picturesque, something deceptively inoffensive, I suppose.

He had come down from the mountain on horseback. He was tall and compelling. Without dismounting, he said he was our neighbor from up the mountain and asked to see the owner of the house. I told him the owner wasn't home, which of course he already knew—he wouldn't have come over otherwise. He might have been drunk; it was early afternoon, in autumn. He took the opportunity to look around the patio and let his horse unload a pile of manure atop the few marigolds that had survived the first frosts of the season. I didn't cry "the marigolds!" although I should have.

"My yellow marigolds!" Although they weren't mine.

"Tell him next time he kills one of my horses I'll set the house on fire," he said before he left.

At four or five in the morning, the same morning I started working as an IKEA shelf-stacker, I heard rumors about our section manager. But when I asked about the rumors, nobody would give me any details. The lady cult kept their distance during the breakfast everyone was so proud of. They clenched their teeth and chewed nonstop. They were proud because the breakfast was free, not too greasy, served in a clean room with the walls painted in warm colors. The moment I saw it, it was obvious to me that all IKEA stores across the world would have the same breakfast room: the same floor plan, the same light fixtures, the same furniture arranged in exactly the same way. This narcotic notion of "pleasantness" was disturbing to me; if, back in Málaga, half-seated on a beach towel with my feet in the sand, I'd had a sneaking suspicion that everything around me was made of painted cardboard, the sea and the song of the water crashing against the coast, then imagine how much worse the feeling was there in the IKEA breakfast room, with the members of the lady cult selecting their pastries and exchanging their thoughts on the latest sale at some department store or another. A little further away, sitting in a beam of yellow light that silhouetted his head perfectly, was an older man—Turkish, judging by his moustache—smoking cigarette after cigarette, every so often submerging the moustache in a cup of coffee. That first morning, he signaled for me to come over. I sat down at his table and he offered me a cigarette, which I accepted, although I don't particularly like to smoke. He observed me for a while as I ate my bread and jam, asking the obligatory questions exchanged like baseball cards between foreigners the world over, feigning interest. He smoked, fasting, and condemned the coffee in hushed tones. I ate my bread and studied the consistency of the jam, no doubt recalling the jars of preserves that had adorned the shelves of the bakery in Heidelberg, the ones customers had asked me for with such desperation, repeating over and over: "A jar of jam, *that* jam! I want to buy it!" And all I could think was: "What on earth is that? A *jar*? Such mysteries . . ." The Turk looked sideways at me. That same day, or maybe the day after, he must have decided that I was of absolutely no use to him.

"What do you mean you threw the chairs, the tablecloth and the lamp into the canal?" Julia screamed at me.

"I couldn't bear to look at them anymore."

"You couldn't bear to look at them!"

Then she caressed my shoulder.

• • •

Let's say you work in a bakery. And a baker comes in. There's no reason for you to tremble. If a baker comes in and he's carrying a tray of croissants, even less reason. Because he's not carrying a knife, or a pistol, or a baseball bat or a shotgun. He's just carrying a tray of croissants. So there's no reason for you suddenly to start trembling like a leaf. But that's how it was. It wasn't fear but rage that made my body shake that way when the baker would come in with his tray of croissants, or empty-handed from out the back, his voice thundering, calling for me.

The policeman insisted I head into town to sleep, but I ignored him. I'd gone into town the day before, and things had not ended well. I looked at his crew cut as he said goodbye, then at the thick iron hand he extended to me.

"I don't understand, why all this effort?" Alexander said when I let slip, as though by chance, that I was looking for a new room to hide my bones in at night. I didn't dare announce it openly to him, preferring to murmur something in the middle of a conversation about the following week's class timetables (let's say), or about the movie we planned to silence ourselves with in a few hours' time. He didn't understand why, so I made up reasons: the neighborhood wasn't central enough, there weren't enough windows in my bedroom, the heating howled in the walls. The next-door neighbors had eyes. On one occasion—the last—he suggested I move into his apartment. We were in the university café, opposite the old main square, where we always met for coffee. Summer or winter, there was always someone sitting on the edge of the fountain. Why won't you look at me? Alexander asked. I certainly hadn't received any better offers: Alexander's apartment was spacious, it had a room that saw the afternoon sun, and that room would be for me. There could be no greater luxury. And the bearings start to move laboriously inside my head, setting a mechanical rhythm, making me believe that a life with Alexander might be possible, a life spent mutually buttering our toast at the breakfast table. What more could a woman hope for? A foreign woman, what's more. Here was a man, poor at first glance, but good at heart—a *European* man, with family somewhere on the Baltic coast and the German state at his back. Alexander knew me well, and tried to explain that this would be a temporary arrangement, purely provisional, that there was no need to worry because as soon as his studies were over we'd be out of there. We'd go wherever I pleased, do whatever I pleased. That night we went to the cinema to see an old movie (French, in all likelihood) which delighted him and bored me half to death. On the screen a woman was crying while some other woman, or maybe a man, insisted "she's crying, she's crying," but in my head, beneath the dry bearings of my thoughts, ideas were circling restlessly. They were all wrong.

It's evening and he comes in and she is in my bedroom, in my house, checking the bed, the wardrobe. And he asks her what she's looking for. And her response must be: "My necklace." Then they hear noises, and he goes to the living room, et cetera.

On a scrap of paper I sketch out the periodic table, with atomic numbers and abbreviations: hydrogen, helium, lithium; H, He, Li. This is a deeply satisfying task. Afterward I look out the window and remember that I am in Buenos Aires, that many years have passed, and I let my gaze wander among the gray rooftops.

I thought about how, if I were to accept Alexander's offer of living together, we would eventually go shopping together, to IKEA or another department store, to find a piece of furniture for a particular corner of the apartment, or a new set of plates and cutlery, or maybe even cups and glasses, the very same ones I'd spent entire mornings stacking onto shelves just a few months ago. And even if it weren't IKEA, even if it were some other emporium, and even if it were curtains instead of glasses, or any other mundane thing—a piece of cling-wrapped meat in the supermarket, that we'd take home and cook on the same stovetop as yesterday, and the day before that, and the week before that. I thought about how it would always and forever more be the same curtains, the same stove, and I told Alexander this, and Alexander said what did it matter if it was the same stove and I didn't answer him because it was a mystery to me too, but a hard one, like a stone hat I was wearing and couldn't take off.

Nevertheless, when we emerged from the cinema I agreed that it was a good film and consented to go for a beer with some of his student friends, all of them approaching or beyond thirty, who like us had wandered lazily out of the cinema and loitered somewhat indecisively on the footpath, not daring to go home. There were two men and a woman. One of them mentioned a café on the Neckar, by the second bridge, so we walked in that direction, taking the avenue that runs along the riverbank. Only when we arrived at the café did I manage to see their faces properly, despite the poor lighting. And although I loved Alexander, and everything about him felt familiar, including his apartment, his love and his furniture, these friends aroused an enormous suspicion in me—one of them in particular. Tall and attentive, he wanted to know why I was working as a sorter of used car parts in a factory forty kilometers away if I'd studied biology and was still able to recite, by heart, the periodic table and the strange secret of morphogenesis. Why didn't I take advantage of the university? Didn't libraries inspire any pity in me? They inspired tremendous pity in me, in fact, libraries and laboratories alike. I would have liked to tell him this in Spanish, in order to express my skepticism with a hint of (perhaps overly facile) irony, but stranded as I was in his linguistic territory I was forbidden the luxury of subtlety and had to settle for a simple "no." We were sitting at a table illuminated by three candles. Beside me, Curious George wanted to know if I had really studied biology or if I was just a teacher, or if I'd in fact dropped out of my degree. As I trawled the menu for coffee liqueur and apple and pear tart he persisted: *was* I a biologist or *was* I a used-car-parts sorter, he asked with visible delight (perhaps he was the one being ironic now). All four of them studied social sciences and reveled in meticulous semantic details, so the conversation advanced along these lines without anyone giving another thought to me or the auto-parts factory or my mysterious past on the other side of the Atlantic. The night's argument had been set in motion, and the biological sample that I represented could now be discarded in a swift antiseptic gesture. Every now and then Alexander caressed my knee under the table, and I let him.

"You should have stayed," chided Julia. Easy for her to say. It was one of those nights of fasting, standing there in the kitchen of her apartment. We'd unintentionally embroiled ourselves, as we often did, in a conversation about extraneous issues that didn't concern us in the slightest, like the fate of the woman who lived across from us, or the new shoe shop that had opened in a neighboring suburb, which we did not intend to frequent. But, like a creeping vine, our conversation eventually curled its way to our own issues, and being women, and enjoying as we did pointless quarrels and the divulging of secrets, we set to reeling off the names and lost intentions of people we hadn't seen in a long time: old friends and lovers. When it was my turn and we got around to the story of Alexander, she told me that, when he'd invited me to live with him all those years ago, back in Heidelberg, I should have accepted immediately, should have moved in that very day, since moving house meant so little to me anyway. Settle in Heidelberg? Wherever, but with him. Because she, Julia, was certain that he'd loved me, and that I—well, what was the alternative? For me it would have been the best thing to do.

"A man who loves you that much . . ."

I was surprised by the sudden lapse into romanticism, so far removed from her usual feminist battles, from the equanimity she so proudly applied when judging the mental hearts of her patients. Julia thought of herself as a practical and sensible person, and here she was arguing that Alexander would have cured me. Of what? Was I unwell? From my symptoms, from my "suitcase syndrome." We arrived at a stalemate, each silently reproaching the other for her lack of understanding. I went to my bedroom and started to prepare my clothes for the next morning: freshly ironed trousers draped over the back of the chair, shirt arranged on top of it, shoes at the foot of the bed. Julia knocked at my door and entered without waiting for a response. She walked a few laps of the room, studied the curtains that fell all the way to the carpet. She said they were dirty and that we could wash them this weekend, if the weather was nice. Then she sat down on the chair and leaned her back against my clothes. What if we went to that party we'd been invited to? A few hours earlier we'd decided against it, but Kolya could always spend the night in the apartment across the hallway, with the old lady and all her oxygen tanks, leaving the two of us free to waste another night of our lives. What harm could it do? Leaving for work early in the morning with bloodshot eyes was a regular practice of ours. I said no, I wanted to sleep. I asked her to please leave. But when she left I didn't put on my pajamas or turn the lights off. I went to the wardrobe and threw all my clothes onto the bed, in great piles and balls, and I pulled the suitcase down from its home on top of the wardrobe and untied the few bags I'd scrunched up behind it. Only when everything was packed up—right down to my ornaments, my two perfumes, my little embroidered wall hanging—did I go to bed. It didn't make sense to get under the covers; it didn't make sense to sleep without them either. But it wasn't the blanket or my anguish or my sadness that kept me from slipping into the warmth of the bed—in fact, I doubt I could have managed to shed a single tear. It was a sense of victory—and who would dare to sleep with victory in their throat?

"This necklace," Madame Cupin said to me one day in her grand dining room, "is an antique treasure my husband brought me from Paris. Nobody knows where I keep it. But I'm telling you, my dear, because I trust you."

Once the last door has closed, once we've survived the last victory, we board a train or a taxi or a tram and we deliver ourselves to an age-old chagrin, forged in gold and silver, that we cherish like a precious coin. The new is always the same.

Back in Argentina, years later, I understood what Julia had tried to tell me. Only two weeks had passed since my arrival at the Del Monje farm in Las Golondrinas, at the foot of the mountain. The house was old-fashioned and smelled of mold. There was a large table in the kitchen, a wood stove and orange furniture from various decades. I'd been promised the house would get cold in winter, and that promise had comforted me; my heart, which is no good, appreciated it. At the back of the house, looking out over hectares of pasture, were the two bedrooms. The kitchen and the living room, filled with glass and plants, looked out onto the patio, toward Marco's house, and, just beyond that, Marco's mother's house. After two weeks on the farm the dogs already knew me, and the cats would meow at me for food. I'd go out to the patio and whoever was about, even if it was just the solitary sheep tied up under the walnut tree, would meander over and ask me, in her own language, for something to eat, as all country animals are wont to do at every opportunity, regardless of whether or not they are actually hungry. The afternoon I finally understood what Julia said to me, I was sitting in the shade of the eaves watching the sheep graze the little strip of grass that constituted her territory. Earlier on, she'd spent a while bleating at me to share with her some of the vegetables I'd just harvested. Before taking them inside I'd thrown her a lettuce leaf, in the hope of cementing our friendship. There were three seeded plots belonging to the Del Monje farm; I saw Marco advancing from the farthest one, the one I never went to. He held the shotgun absently in his hand, as though it were a stick or a rope. He came toward me and leaned the shotgun on the patio, instead of going to his house and putting it away as I'd seen him do once before. Smiling, he asked me if I was enjoying the work and if the peas were green yet; I answered yes to both questions. I invited him to sit down in the empty chair, in the shade, instead of standing in the sun looking at me without even shielding his eyes. He ignored me and kept talking about the vegetables that would be ready to harvest tomorrow or the next day, and how we should divide the work with the farmhand: who would pick the broad beans and who the raspberries. Such matters interested me less and less, and as he spoke I concentrated on savoring the details of his face, his gestures, his whole presence. What about the chilies? And the basil? What did I know. Again I offered him a chair, but he murmured something and went over to the tap to wash his hands and arms. It was hot, that end-of-summer heat. Only after he'd washed did he accept my offer of a chair and a glass of water, which I fetched from inside. As I walked over to give him the water I saw that his shirt was stained. I mentioned this, and he replied that it was possible he'd got blood on it because he'd just shot a horse. I recoiled. Which horse? The neighbor's horse. The blond one? That's what I called him, because he had a long gold-and-ocher mane. The blond one, yeah. Clean shot to the heart, so it wouldn't suffer. Now the animal lay sleeping in the tall maize.

During my two weeks at the farm I'd ventured to pat the blond horse through the fence several times, and I'd fed him two apples, which he'd received with a grateful whinny. And now his blood was fertilizing the soil beneath the maize. I studied Marco as he drank his glass of water and I tried to loathe him, him and the awful bloodstains that traced little designs on his clothes. But I couldn't, and then I realized that Julia had been right, all those years ago.

In the afternoon, for example, if I was in my bedroom listening to music or reading some teen magazine, my father would poke his head in to tell me he was heading out, and after confirming that the sun was coming in through the bedroom window he'd ask me if I knew it was only the afternoon because we were orbiting a very bright star at sixteen hundred kilometers per hour, rotating all the while on our own axis. It's not correct to say *it's the afternoon*, he'd point out. It was nothing but a very bright star and a planetary body completing its elliptical circuit, the inhabitants of which, at some point, had invented the concept of post meridiem repose. And with that he'd blow me a kiss and leave, feeling satisfied with himself.

Of all the breads in the Heidelberg bakery, the best-selling ones were the rye and the poppy-seed rolls. Despite their proven popularity, they were always relegated to the hardest-to-reach shelves. There was no good reason for this: that much I understood immediately. I touched the label that read *rye*, I touched the label that read *poppy seed*. Neither was fixed in its place. I switched them with the labels that read *sesame*. Then I switched them back.

"Sunflower seed?" I asked, because the sunflower-seed rolls were the easiest to reach. "No, rye," or "No, poppy seed," the customers said, every time. And since there was no ladder I'd have to stand on top of an upturned basket and try not to lose my balance. One morning I saw the baker emerging from out the back, tall and wrapped up in his apron. He didn't even look at me. He headed straight for the shelves and, barely stretching his arms, delivered the loaves of rye and poppy seed into the farthest corner. I could have said something, but my tongue had retreated into the back of my throat months ago.

The next day he discovered my existence, and began to order me around. Although I'd been assigned to front of house in the bakery, and sometimes the owner would even crown me with a white bonnet and ask me to serve in the adjoining patisserie, that morning the baker decided to use me to his advantage. He liked the word "use"—he used it all the time. He'd say, this is useful, this is not useful, and wave his utensils in the air, or loaves of bread that had turned out to be defective. He'd make some gesture at me, a silent nod of the head maybe, and take me into the back room where the ovens and other machinery were. The mixing machines fascinated me, like giant sea monsters. But I wasn't allowed to linger, nor was I to examine the bread paddles, or the shiny buttons. I was there to carry the hot trays and take them out the front, I was there to powder the croissants and doughnuts with icing sugar. "The spatula!" the baker would yell from the corner. The spatula! The comb! The yeast! I didn't know what those things were. I'd run from one side of the room to the other, never daring to touch any of the utensils or ingredients. Meanwhile, the baker's apprentice was bored to death at the front counter, with his dry skin and his sunken eyes. But there I was running around in circles as the baker demanded the spatula, the flour, the apron. The baker mumbled, he moaned and nagged. He asked me for the paddle and the spatula, and he received neither. But not once did he attempt to teach me anything. He was very good at ensuring I remained ignorant, grumbling all the while in his mysterious language. He'd send me back out the front with a tray and then, knowing full well that I could hear him, yell: "She doesn't even know what flour is!" Once he'd confirmed that I also didn't know what yeast was, or a comb, or an apron, he'd gesture for me to leave, and the apprentice would return to his usual job. The scene repeated itself often, and after the baker had finally grown tired of me and sent me back to the front counter he'd re-emerge, a little while later, like the lanky animal he was, and walk through the bakery into the patisserie where they sold the cakes and pastries, and make a show of berating his small wife. She would invariably remain calm, and eventually he'd return grumbling to the back of the bakery. It was a slow war the baker had decided to wage against me, and against his wife, who was a firm believer in the benefits of employing foreigners. In the afternoons he'd come over with a very serious expression on his face and ask me for the money from the till. He'd force me to perform rapid-fire calculations as he dictated big numbers to me, numbers with zeros and commas, which rained down on my head like a stream of in-sects and were incomprehensible to me. He persisted anyway, of course, with his five-hundred-and-eighty-seven-euros-and-forty-three-cents, and all the rest. And I—I who had dreamed of mathematics back in Buenos Aires, when I grew tired of biology—was suddenly incapable of distinguishing thirty-two from twenty-three.

The fire was a signature. It wound its way up the side of the mountain like a slow footprint, feigning capriciousness. It was February. Marco had gone out very early that morning, on horseback, without a word. Such expeditions were not unusual, although he was careful to avoid them if the weather was too warm. But this morning already promised a high and solitary sun, harsh in its nakedness. At midday I went out to the patio to watch the fire, which I could only just make out in the distance. As afternoon descended, it became more visible. By evening, when Marco returned, it had transformed into a long bright flourish, eating up the patient pines and cypresses, along with a good chunk of the old fruit trees that belonged to our alcoholic neighbor—the one Marco had argued with about the water that time. Marco arrived covered in dirt, his clothes a little singed on the chest and legs. He told me they'd been fighting the fire and asked me to feed his horse, which smelled three times worse than usual. I saw him leaving the house later, and went over to him. His face was different, it belonged to someone else; those were not his eyes. He refused to look at me, didn't say a word. I lay down in the house, alone. The rooms were barely beginning to cool down after an exhausting summer's day. I thought: Marco didn't go out to fight a fire that morning; he went out to start one.

If I stay, I stay. If I go, I go. This thought was soothing in the beginning, but then it wasn't anymore. In the beginning I'd just think something logical, and it would calm me down. In the beginning I'd just say "it's logical," and I'd feel perfectly fine. I moved around logically, from one new city to the next, one new bedroom to the next. And it worked the other way, too: if I stayed, I stayed because it was rational to do so. But soon my reasons grew, like a big bouquet. In Berlin and Heilbronn I spent my time contemplating all those rational flowers, morning and night. I call them flowers, but I am suspicious of my own words; if I'd really had a bouquet of reasons, I would have wanted to count them and pull all their petals off. But my reasons had no petals, and no perfume.

"*Camellia sinensis*," I said to Alexander the day I met him. Something unprecedented had occurred in the university café in Heidelberg, the one opposite the main square: they'd run out of coffee, and the disconcerted students—among whom Alexander, tall and brown-haired, wasn't particularly eye-catching—milled about in confusion. I'd squandered my time so effectively since arriving in that city that I was incapable of the most basic communication; I didn't even know that tea, in their language, was simply called "tea." Or maybe I was just nervous, caught off guard by the crowds and the racket.

"*Camellia sinensis*," I said the minute he sat down at the table beside me, when I noticed that his white cup bore tea instead of coffee. So began our first conversation. Alexander laughed and pointed to a flower printed at the top of the menu; it could have been a daisy, or perhaps some kind of marigold: "*Calendula officinalis*," I ventured. Suddenly he was happy. He pointed at a ficus tree growing with difficulty against the window: "*Ficus benjamina*," I replied. It took us a little while to realize we had

Spanish in common; he, at least, seemed German, and I had always been hard to categorize, like a stray dog.

"Camellia?" he persevered. I played along one more time.

His expression changed as he sipped his *camellia sinensis*. He said hello to a couple of students who stopped as they passed by our table, pretending he didn't know me, as if we hadn't just been exchanging Latin words and smiles. When his friends left he went back to his tea and studied me with his eyes. For half an hour, three quarters, a full hour he didn't say a word, submerged in a book that lay to one side of his teacup. He also looked out the window for a while. It was neither snowy nor sunny, but the Heidelberg summer was over and the encroaching autumn was anything but benign. I was afraid, as if from a distance, of the long nights winter was beginning to promise.

But with Marco, back in Argentina, in the house on the mountain, I didn't need any of those words. From the very first, the orchards I worked in had left me mute. I no longer cared about Latin names or vegetable families or the nervation of leaves, or photosynthesis or mitochondria or covalent bonds. If I felt tired, I'd sit down on a tree stump and stretch out my legs; if I felt hungry, I'd steal a couple of strawberries, wash and eat a carrot; if I felt cold, I'd rug up; if I felt tired . . . et cetera. And with Marco it was the same, right from the beginning, right from that very first afternoon when I arrived at the Del Monje farm and followed the dirt trail through the gates and gave a little round of applause. The next day he let me work in the strawberry field with the other harvesters, and when the strawberries began to grow scarce we switched to collecting pods and separating peas. I never knew how the earth could provide such happiness, and perhaps I still don't know, but that's how it seems to me, and that's what I believe. For once I wasn't thinking about coleoptera or pollinating agents. Marco would give us orders and then disappear, on horseback or on foot, into the neighboring fields. He'd return without warning and wander around in silence. We'd see him again at the end of the day, inside the house, where he'd pay us our wages. The day I saw him farewelling the summer renters, I asked him if there were any rooms available. Just as the weather began to turn sour I moved into the little house. I'd been away from home for ten years, my father was dead. I had no family left, except for my brothers, both of whom, under the guise of their daily lives, were still striving in their own way for a melancholy kind of normality. When I'd arrived back in Buenos Aires the first thing they'd asked me was: what was that about, all those years abroad? And my father, most definitely dead. But Marco didn't want to know any of this when I arrived at the Del Monje farm and moved into the little house, the one between his house and his mother's house, with the walnut tree spilling over the patio. It would get cold in winter, he told me. And that had comforted me, like a happy promise.

Under a marquee in the bazaar, a man sells me a sweet in the shape of a green heart.

In Heidelberg, however, the cold was foreign and I didn't like the snow, it became bland very quickly. Buried beneath pyramids of hats and scarves everybody seemed diseased, and suspicious of everyone else's disease. I'd get up at three in the morning, sometimes two-thirty, and wash and moisturize my face, then head out into the darkness to arrive at IKEA at four. The Turk was always standing at the entrance smoking with his eyes half-closed, occasionally chewing his moustache. He'd ignore us all if we waved at him and never, no matter how bitter and wretched the cold, no matter how damp and gloomy, did he wear a hat or beanie. I'd made a lot of promises in my IKEA job that I was unable to keep: everyone else seemed to like their uniforms with the yellow logo, but I didn't; everyone else was happy with the breakfast, but I wasn't; nobody else complained about the music, but I did, silently. Sometimes I'd simply exclaim: "This music!" without using a verb, which would have been risky, and without committing to any particular intonation, because whenever I said this someone, usually one of the members of the lady cult or one of the younger employees, would reply: "What music?" And if I pointed it out they'd say, "Ah, yes, isn't it lovely?" Every now and then the cult ladies would advise me that I should be afraid. Of a glass? Yes, a broken glass was something to be feared. The boss who was my boss, even though I'd never seen her, was coming just after breakfast, and even though I'd hidden the three broken glasses, and the plate, the cult ladies knew about them. During breakfast I'd smoked a cigarette with the mustachioed man. He hid his cigarette after each drag. I smoked openly, trembling, with a certain languor. But I wasn't afraid of being afraid—not then, not since. The boss was a blonde, short-haired woman. She wore a scarf around her neck and a thick layer of makeup on her face, in a poor attempt at disguising her age. In her world I did not exist, but the Turk did. When the time came, he was called by his only name: "Turk!

Come here!" The mustachioed man, hunched at that moment over a pile of blankets not far from where I stood, left his basket and walked placidly toward the kitchenware section. I'm not sure if they spoke about the broken glasses. My tongue, as we all know, was still asleep in its Spanish dream. I continued squashing cushions. When the Turk came back he said to me as he passed: "Modern slavery." He suddenly seemed a thousand years old. The supervisor had started screaming because the customers would be entering the store in two minutes and we had to turn ourselves into ghosts before anyone saw us, we had to disappear immediately. "Let's go, ghosts!" she screamed. The Turk helped me with the remaining cushions, which were many. "It's already ten o'clock!" she persisted. We needed to vanish. "None of you exist!" sang the supervisor. And he resisted, he was the last one to disappear. I noticed this with pleasure, because by then I knew already that my heart was cut from bad cloth.

I said to Julia when I got the chance, posted there behind the espresso machine, where every so often a customer would come and interrupt me, that seven years had passed since I'd left Buenos Aires to live, first in Madrid, then in Almagro, Málaga, Heilbronn and Heidelberg, and now in Berlin. I told her I'd never managed to stay in any of those places, never even managed to stay in one room for very long, because the *people*, because the *doors*, the *windows*. When I said this she smiled at me very kindly and assured me from the other side of the espresso machine that in Berlin all of this wandering would come to an end, that with her help I'd find something worth staying for, a home with a street name and number.

"Come and visit us at home sometime," she said. "You'll love Kolya."

I wanted to reply that the mere presence of a three-year-old child in any house was motive enough for me to avoid it entirely, even in my imagination, but who could say such a thing to a mother, standing there behind an espresso machine in the midst of all those interruptions; who could speak such a sentence, even if it were true? Not me. I lied to her and said I'd love to, so that she'd leave, with the intention of inventing some excuse later on, but Julia was inordinately pleased and started talking about Kolya with such compassion, telling me that he was a solitary child, a child who needed a lot of affection, that he'd been abandoned, that he was suffering, et cetera. Julia leaves and I am left to attend to other customers. Julia left a while ago and I am cleaning the coffee machine. The next day I make good on my promise and become acquainted with the house by the canal. I watch Kolya playing with a ball. I believe that I hate Kolya, that I hate Julia. But this is false.

It's getting late and I see one last sun reflected in the steel of the axe, which has been left lying on its side, although the patio is clean. It's strange to see it there. I wonder if I should put it away. But I suppose Marco knows what he's doing. Everything he does is in accordance with his own personal set of procedures, of that I'm certain. To feed or to destroy, horse or tree. He silently passes judgment on the life and death of every paddock, every sheep left standing. Watching him cut wood or pull up a plant is the same as understanding a very complicated formula, or a long chemical reaction.

My father, who after my mother's death dedicated himself to physics with ludicrous subservience, had a habit of rejecting things. I did not have this habit, but then I learned it from him. So does that mean I also had a habit of rejecting things? I was in kindergarten when she died, and since that time, or perhaps even before, I'd received the occasional lecture on scientific negation from my father. These lectures were never scheduled, never announced in advance; like all early education they were mixed in with my food and drink, imparted incidentally and without a great deal of insistence. He simply enjoyed tainting with doubt everything I was beginning to believe. The blue of the sky? Just an effect of the Earth's atmospheric gases and the light of the sun. And out there, in space, the temperature was two hundred and seventy degrees below zero. And if we looked at the sun we'd be burned alive. He didn't do this to instill in me some kind of premature skepticism, nor to destroy the edifice of my child's happiness with the crushing blows of his sarcasm. He was naive with his wisdom, a well-intentioned butcher of innocence. On the weekends we'd go canoeing on the river and get ice cream on Avenida Maipú. The cars we saw racing by were converting chemical energy into kinetic energy, and the trees were also using gravity to stay still because, even though they had roots, without gravity they would all be floating in the sky. At night I would dream, inevitably, of floating trees.

We unhung the curtains and washed them. It was Sunday, there was plenty of time and sunshine. Berlin looked like a mammal outstretched in the sun. And yet in my throat there was a stone.

The baker also had a habit of rejecting things, in his way. When I first started my job in the bakery I'd tremble when I heard his voice thundering my name from a distance. But as the months went by I began to wish for it: for him to treat me unfairly, to provoke me with his comments, like the time I refused to unload the freshly baked bread with my bare hands and he told me the heat burning my fingers was purely psychological.

"You don't understand anything," he said, the ignorant shit, and some part of me enjoyed telling him he was right. Because—I've said it before—my heart is no good. He despised the pastry chef, and loved to disavow both the difficulty of cakes and the advantages of democracy. He wasn't old, but if he had been, once upon a time he would have used his arms to carry guns and kill Jews and Gypsies. His father had also been a baker. He was a kind old man who came by every now and then, grandson in tow, to admire the handiwork of his successor. I was a bit saddened by their little family, but as the months went by I got used to it. I'd arrive at work early, when it was still dark, and meticulously arrange the jars of jam without knowing what they were called, nor which fruits they were made of. I'd stack them up into towers and the order of it all gave me a certain confused kind of joy. Then the apprentice would appear from out the back, all wrapped up in an apron, and unload a torrent of bread rolls onto the farthest shelf. At ten past six the garbage man would arrive, a giant who barked his riddle at me once or twice and, in an act of compassion, finally showed me which bread he wanted by pointing at it. I pronounced the prices fearfully, playing the language like an out-of-tune violin. But I liked my job, and it was enough for me, although back at home—which is to say, back in my room, which could have been any room—my legs would hurt when I lay down to sleep. First it was weeks and then months, and my heart got its hopes up; finally it thought it was worth something.

The past: that long and sensible mistake. For years I knew I was making a mistake, but always I took the hardest path. That used to redeem me. Not anymore.

I was traveling south to the harvest. It was November. Why, if I'd never shown any interest in the countryside before now? I fled from my brother's house one night with nothing but a hiker's backpack. At least, I thought I was fleeing; in reality, nobody was chasing me. I pretend-fled from Retiro, after not sleeping a wink in the traveler's hotel, on a bus headed for El Bolsón. I lived in the cabin in the gully. Then I moved to the little house in the middle of the Del Monje farm where Marco was, to put it sentimentally, let's say "waiting for me." At the beginning he didn't speak (he didn't speak much later on, either) but that was his way. Sometimes he supervised, sometimes he killed horses, while we harvesters plucked strawberries and raspberries in the fields. I'd made the house in the middle of the farm my own. He never said more than three words at a time: seems that way; gotta be done; there's no need. I watched him from my window if I was in the house, or from the field if I was working and he was passing by to check the fruit baskets. And although I didn't quite understand why—despite the cold and the hard labor, despite the twitching in my legs when I'd lie down on the battered mattress each night, despite Madame

Cupin pacing the patio with her walking stick—with time I started to grow sweetly still, as if under the effect of beautiful music. One day, during the siesta hour, I realized that Marco's mother had been observing me from the veranda of her wooden house as keenly as I observed Marco and the black-muzzled sheep. She was always hunched over with her back to the patio, removing any new weeds that had crept into her garden. In December the first tourists admired her from afar, as if she were just one more attraction. They'd avoid her and approach me, so that I could show them the berry orchards and sell them fruit. As I wrapped up their purchases they'd asked me not about the secrets of agriculture but about that old woman: what an outfit! What a magnificent garden! They admired Madame Cupin, and I suspected nothing: she seemed by turns sweet and malicious. One day she appeared at my house, knocked on the front door and said to me from the porch: "So when are you coming over to visit me, young lady?" As if we'd arranged the visit some time ago. She smelled of perfume, and the wrinkles on her face were just one more embellishment of the impeccably cultivated figure she cut. I'm sure she took them off at night, as she did her rings and pearl necklaces. I'm sure she was twenty-five years old when she closed her eyes in bed. She was captivating, much more so than the sheep with the black muzzle and the walnut tree bent over the patio.

I had as many pieces as a broken vase, and I never found a way to put them back together or even to number my porcelain remains. If I'd at least been able to feel pity, to sing like Julia or fight like Alexander with his liberty conundrum. But instead I studied a green beetle, or went out silently on tiptoe to feed the cats. I didn't think, and even this wasn't any comfort.

In the café by the main square, in Heidelberg, just a few blocks from where I'd worked with the baker selling poppy-seed loaves, it was a pleasure to sit and talk with Alexander and linger for hours inside the little cave that was, for us, the Spanish language. He had originally learned the language in its homeland, but luckily he'd met a number of exiled Ecuadorians, Chileans and Peruvians and now spoke a mellower, more deliberate version. More and more frequently, we ended up whiling away our afternoons together: first an hour, then another hour. And he touched my knee underneath the table. He had only recently returned from one of those trips he took "to think." And, just like the other times, he refused to speak about it, telling me instead about his university classes and the usual trivialities of student life, knowing full well I was not interested in any of it, although sometimes, for my benefit, he did mention his basic knowledge of chemistry and botany. The abracadabra of *camellia sinensis* had long since stopped working. Alexander (who, as a European, dreamed of becoming a citizen of the world) dedicated himself uncomplainingly to the social sciences. But at thirty-five he had already grown weary of skepticism. His critical faculties were beginning to falter, along with his hopeful spirit. He no longer doubted, as he had in his twenties, the existence of God and institutions. He was beginning to dethrone certain books and genuinely consider the kinds of jobs that would require him to pay taxes. I'm not saying he was ready to throw in the towel and clamber inside the infinite rodent wheel; even in his mid-thirties he was still fiercely protective of his liberty. He'd go from the library to his apartment, from the apartment to his night classes. The afternoons when he deviated from routine were spent with me in the café. The life he'd cultivated was the life of a public servant. Why do I speak so spitefully of Alexander, even though I loved him? Is it *because* I loved him? My heart has not improved with time, despite the goodness of Carmen and the goodness of Julia, despite Alexander and all our sex, despite Marco and his death. If anything, it's worse. I thought I was getting better when all the while I was getting worse. Because back then all I saw was a young man with a thirst for knowledge, Europe weighing heavily on one shoulder (the other shoulder he believed to be free), who wanted to spend his nights with me. I went along with it, went home with him and let him take off my clothes and admire my body. Then all subtleties were done away with, because he was a surgeon of sex, a precious alchemist, with all the patience of a good botanist. I saw how the whole European continent weighed down on one of his shoulders even after he'd removed his suit of civility. Naked and simian, he was still a child of the West, and he admitted as much himself: I am a child of Europe and the West, he'd say, and it was only by following the path of the West that one could attain the liberty he prized above all else. He was convinced that in order to think about liberty one needed, first, to be free and to practice freedom, as though it were a violin sonata or a martial art. He went to the Black Forest and he returned from the Black Forest. It was one of his central practices. He'd leave somewhat downcast and return barely smiling. He'd return and settle back into his apartment as if nothing had happened, ask for and receive sex, ask for and receive food, consume books as if it were utterly natural. He took large sips of everyday life, and invited me to take sips too, insisting in his velvety Spanish: "vamos, venga, bebe," and I'd accept, under the illusion that I was drinking a magic potion.

In the ABB factory, about forty kilometers outside Heidelberg, I argue with a Polish man who crosses the border to work when he's short on money—the rest of the time, he studies at the University of Warsaw. He tells me I'm a good slave, that I'm not helping the cause. First I'm offended, then I defend myself; much later, I concede defeat.

I tried explaining it to Julia in the Berlin kitchen. For her, a person's life was an argument filled with hidden meanings and *causalities*, and she enjoyed discovering them and inventing them as we stood there by the kitchen bench, nibbling on a piece of bread or fruit, as I've already explained, on those long evenings when we'd decide to abstain from dinner, with Kolya sleeping in the other room, and we'd peck and chatter like two birds, and so on. That night, like so many others, it was at Julia's request that we started talking about Alexander and everything that had gone wrong between us. But now she didn't react the way she usually did, with a sideways glance and her hand over her mouth every time she commented or responded. "Why not, if you loved him?" she half-offered, distracted, examining the teeth beneath her cheek. What was that? A red mark to one side of her mouth. She confessed that earlier that day someone had punched her in the face. It was the day of her hospital shift—the rest of the week she worked in the clinic. To see Julia behind her black teak desk, surrounded by framed paintings, under that soft lighting, as I saw her once, was to trust her immediately and completely. Julia seemed to embody the consecration of understanding, like some kind of patron saint of psychoanalysts, if such a thing could exist. She was so regal, so inscrutable at times, although she believed in love and happiness; and yet someone had punched her in the face so hard that one of her teeth had come loose, an incisor, just to the left of her smile. As the hours passed the red mark got worse. She touched it constantly, refused to put ice on it. A week had passed since I'd packed my suitcases in victory, but I was still hanging around as if nothing had happened, which, some might say, is exactly what did happen. I'd packed my suitcases and locked them before hiding them away on the highest shelf of the wardrobe. It had been difficult to lift them, heavy as they were, that insomniac night. During the week I'd contrived not to open them again, to survive with nothing but the clothes on my back, and I still harbored hopes of leaving and putting an end to it all. Even to Julia? Yes: putting an end to Julia, and Kolya, and Alexander and the memory of him; putting an end to doña Carmen, to Almagro and Málaga and Heilbronn, and even my own father, who had died, or so I'd been told, exactly one day before; throwing a thick blanket of disdain over all of it and setting out like a new person to see new men and new buildings, with the same joys and woes, to find new jobs and new rooms and feel new winds blowing at my back. The Caribbean or the Russian steppe, cleaning bathrooms or safeguarding paintings in a museum, or shampooing dogs, or selling ice cream in a marketplace. It's not like it was all the same to me, but what was I to do? All things bright and reinvigorating, all of it brought me hope. And that night we ate on our feet as we often did, an apple and a piece of black bread as we exchanged our thoughts on the progress of the apartment building's internal patio, which was in the process of being painted white, or the neighbor across the hallway and her illness. But Julia spoke sideways and without enthusiasm, and she didn't even reproach me when I said I'd never known how to really love anyone. No, this time she didn't speak to me with her usual authority, she kept her mouth half-closed and a restless hand to her cheek. Did I want to know what had happened? Was it possible that I didn't even care? I cared about the ice she'd refused to apply, and the makeup she'd need the next day. A woman had punched her in the face during a struggle; they were trying to tranquilize her, and the woman had resisted. The punch had been administered very precisely, its effect exacerbated by a sharp metal ring. A woman had hit her like a man. She, Julia, who was pure understanding, who was the patron saint of the mentally ill, who believed in explanations and the happiness of others. "We were trying to help her. We had a plan." The woman had thrown punches in all directions at first, but she'd managed to hit Julia with graphic precision, like sticking a pin through her lip. Ah, Julia. Her understanding had hit rock bottom, and as she told me about the punch she traced its memory time and time again across her cheek.

"Don't worry, they'll be back."

"Who?"

"The bad things," said one of the brothers from the cabins, with a subtle tone of sorrow. He had come down to the farm to buy cherries because his tree had been attacked by a patient and diligent worm. He pulled the worm from his pocket and showed it to me. We talked about his fruit trees and cursed the fire that had burned down the neighbor's orchard a few days ago. He slung a few more sentences at me before taking his leave with a wink. He had no desire to intimidate me. I could tell that more than one of the mountain dwellers believed Marco had fanned the flames instead of extinguishing them.

"We're never still. Even rest is a kind of movement," I told a man a few months ago, a man lying prostrate and still in his bedroom. An old, sick man. His hands and feet were useless to him.

Do I mean my father? Maybe. I must have said this to my father over the telephone, from seventeen thousand kilometers away. It was a Thursday. The next day he died, and Julia came home with a broken mouth.

"You," bellowed Madame Cupin one afternoon as she made her way toward my little house. I'd been living at the Del Monje farm for six months, under the nose of the now-snowy mountain. "Am I mistaken, or did I tell you where I kept my pearls? Because I've been looking for them and I can't find them anywhere."

From the beginning of Julia's story I understood the woman's reasons for punching her. With such precision, according to Julia, like the exact opposite of a caress. I too had dreamed of slaps and punches, more than once. One for the baker in Heidelberg, who threw numbers at me and made them rain down upon my head. One for my boss in the big department store. One for my father. One for a certain organic chemistry textbook, that I ended up throwing out the window. Not the kind of slap reserved for wiping out insolence, but a properly placed fist, something painful. The crazy woman, Julia said, had been possessed by some kind of maniacal strength; she hadn't reacted to the needle the nurse brandished but rather to Julia's declaration that they were only there to help. "We have a plan," Julia had said, and one of those words had provoked the punch to her mouth, unless it had been the magic wand of the word "help." Once her hands were tied down the woman had yelled *no*. So easy, those crazies, it didn't take much brainpower to understand them. I saw Julia with new eyes then. She was too pretty to be hit. But then again, why not? Throw a punch at the mouth of beauty. The woman's hands were tied and she was dragged down the corridor like a blood clot, like a drifting planet, bouncing from wall to wall, all the way to her cell.

When we worked as IKEA shelf-stackers, we *were* IKEA shelf-stackers. We behaved like obedient planets each spinning in our own orbit, according to the gravitational laws of our boss. From kitchenware to interior decoration, from the arrangement of plates to sheets, via every imaginable prerequisite for the perfect European home. But not the Turk. What was his name? Fatik? Who knows. I hated that they called him the Turk, and yet I too called him the Turk. A new girl had just started, from Ukraine or Latvia. Very blonde, insipidly so. She didn't join the lady cult, nor did she seem to want to have anything to do with me, but she adored the Turk and sometimes, if he allowed it, she'd even bludge a cigarette off him during the break and stroke his moustache. They got along very well; naturally, it didn't take long for tongues to start wagging. I saw the pair convening for a moment in the morning, as we entered the building to arrange whatever it was we were asked to arrange that day. During breakfast they winked and made somewhat unnecessary signs at one another, since aside from me nobody was the least bit interested in what they had to say. When they spoke they spoke badly of the Germans, in bad German. The Germans were this and that, and our boss epitomized every one of those faults. I agreed with every point they made, but I didn't dare tell them that. Sometimes, when our paths crossed at the break table, they'd share the odd ironic observation with me, usually something borderline crude, and make some gesture so that I'd understand. After the forging of their alliance, more broken glasses began to appear, more frayed mattresses. At first they were subtle about it, and it was fun to speculate about the precise moment when they slipped away to perpetrate their crimes. They might have spent long and precious months this way—for her they were certainly precious, and for the Turk even more so. While he continued to smoke his ascetic's cigarette every morning by the access door, still refusing to don scarf or beanie, it now seemed he spent the whole day wrestling with an enormous and secret happiness. Since he was nearly fifty, and I was only twenty-five, I imagined that this newfound happiness must be something like a rallying against time, the recovery of something lost. I was wrong. I saw them ripping the ears off a couple of teddy bears imported from China. Always just two or three, be it bears or glasses: a series of artfully faked accidents. Their sabotage was meager, in the scheme of things, and they knew it, but they took pleasure in it all the same, for a time. They never invited me to participate, and even if they had I would have refused; my heart wasn't hardy enough for such things. They might have kept up the ruse for months, but she got anxious. It was she, not he, who must have insisted on taking it a step further.

Sometimes, after making love, Alexander would stroke my hair as if I were a dog.

And I was a dog.

I saw her silhouetted against the backdrop of trees, behind the house. She was struggling to remove her stiff leg from the mud. It had been raining day and night for several days and nights. It was the beginning of autumn and I wasn't afraid of the cold or the snow which, somewhere, was already starting to gestate. Her leg was calf-deep in the mud and her walking stick had sunk even deeper. One of the cats observed her from its post with ominous indifference. I confess that I didn't rush to her aid. Like the cat, I watched her from a distance for a moment before approaching her. She was so elegant, even there in the mud. She struggled alone, grabbing at a branch that was within her reach; she wouldn't let me get my shoes dirty. Once she was free we walked together to the front porch of her house, commenting on the volatile weather, which had already claimed a number of plants in her garden. She disappeared inside for a few minutes to get changed and returned as fresh as a daisy, smelling of rosewater. The living and dining rooms surprised me: it was the first time I'd seen antique furniture and high ceilings in a place as remote as Las Golondrinas. Madame Cupin noticed my reaction and informed me that her second marriage had been to a Frenchman—a lover of classical architecture and gambling. Thirty years ago he'd arranged for the entire contents of a family estate he'd inherited to be shipped over. Now widowed, Marco's mother drifted past the old ornate mirrors like a ghost from a bygone era, although the veneer of elegance had its cracks: her walking stick was cheap and crude, and the whisky she offered me was local. I took two sips and set it aside. Constantly shifting her bad leg, she asked me if I'd enjoyed the harvest and—when I complimented her interior decoration—whether I'd visited the Continent. I answered yes to both questions. I tried to avoid speaking about my past in any depth, but she was interested in my family, my parents, their professions; in short, she was keen to unravel the fabric of my origins. I ceded a little information and she paused a while to share the little she knew about chemistry and biology. Monsieur Cupin had been a man of great culture, she told me, although I hadn't seen a single book inside that impressive house. She took a sip of whisky and started to muse on the paltry benefits of my working for the local health-food shop, which I did in order to pay the rent that she and her son charged me. She advised me to quit: she didn't like those people (which people?). Before I took my leave she told me she'd resigned herself to the fact that her son would be alone forever. Marriage just wasn't for him.

"Marco is just too good, you see."

She shook my hand and gave me a slow kiss on the cheek. When I got to the back door it was already dark outside, and I bumped into something on my way out.

"Ah, the axe," I heard her say. "Lately he's been leaving it lying around any old place."

Kolya was hugging my leg. We were alone. Julia had gone out and I'd just given him something bland and mashed to eat. I reached down and stroked his yellow hair, which always reminded me of summer. I looked into his Russian eyes. I felt nothing.

His situation was different to mine; all I knew was flight. But if Marco was planning something, anything, I didn't see it. He was too tied to his life on the mountain, happily tied down. Where would he possibly have gone to make a new life for himself? He'd leave early in the morning, with or without bridle in hand, and remain silent for days and weeks at a time. Once I worked up the courage to tell Madame Cupin. She didn't seem to think anything of it. She just smiled her centuries-old condescending smile.

"He's a mysterious one," she said, leaning on her walking stick. "He's probably working on a business deal, or else he's got some woman on the side. Don't worry, it never lasts long."

The names of the implements in the Heidelberg bakery remained unknown to me until my final day of work. The baker always made sure to demand them in his own language, without ever explaining which one he was referring to, without making so much as a gesture, or deigning to show me the slightest bit of goodwill. He'd launch a word into the air like a bright firecracker and watch me run from one end of the kitchen to the other in search of something useful-looking. Then he'd distract me, or somehow procure the dough-cutter or comb in secret, behind my back, and complain about my poor attention span and lack of skill. He'd come over when

I was at the cash register and ask me for money, making his numbers rain on my head. The afternoon of the furious customer came about like this: we were about to close up shop. I'd been working in the bakery for four months, and had managed to gather up enough reasons and savings to justify quitting. I figured I'd look for another job, play the role of the well-behaved foreigner in some other neck of the woods. Something had signaled the direction of my next flight. I'd been through the obligatory night of brutal self-honesty ("stop lying to yourself, it's time to go") and experienced a vision of the future: a perfectly white, empty page. And yet that afternoon, when the furious customer stormed into the Heidelberg bakery, I didn't move an inch. The customer was yelling that his delivery had been a disaster: *kaput!* Later on I learned the details: a series of blunders that extended all the way from the late delivery to the dismal state of the canapés. His party had been a total failure. *Kaput!* What about the desserts? Same thing. And the cream was rancid. The baker himself had been the one to prepare the delivery. He'd stayed late the night before to work on it. I knew this because he'd spent half the morning complaining that he hadn't had enough sleep. But when the customer made a dash for the counter and tried to force his way into the back of the bakery, I said there was nobody there (a simple enough sentence in German) and that the failed delivery had been my fault (this last point I made stammeringly, pointing at my own chest to clarify). I'm not sure if he understood my scrappy gibberish. He said he'd be back. The baker was still out the back, hidden away in his sanctuary, when I finished mopping the floors and turned out the lights. I called "see you tomorrow" and he didn't answer. I left, promising myself that I wouldn't come back the next day, already regretting the ignoble sacrifice I'd just made. What was the point, I wondered, footsteps and tears falling on the pavement. I had no love for myself. I was good for nothing. But this bad heart of mine, which is neither fair nor kind, trembled happily there beneath my shoulder.

It's not true that we leave a place when the future is adorned with beautiful visions of faraway travels. We leave one morning, the morning after any given evening, or the afternoon after any given midday, just when we'd decided to stay forever.

"Name?"

I gave it to him.

"Profession?"

In the past, I would have tangled myself up in long explanations trying to answer this question. I told him I worked for the local health-food shop, which he already knew. He noted everything down diligently, with a rather tortuous hand, on a paper form that didn't look very official. I didn't glimpse so much as an old typewriter, let alone anything resembling a screen—nothing, in other words, to remind us that we had advanced beyond the analogue age. He sat on one side of the desk and I sat on the other, and we played our respective roles well. The little room we were in had faulty doors and a tiled floor, and three large flies buzzed over our heads like a ceiling fan. How long had I known the deceased? And the second victim, Mrs. Cupin? I explained that I'd arrived at the Del Monje farm one year ago, to work on the harvest, and had decided to stay. Why? It would have taken me half a lifetime to answer that question. I threw him an excuse like small change, knowing it wasn't enough. The interrogation followed a course I'd rather not have taken, but there was nothing to be done about it. When did you last see them? At the Hotel Amancay, I said. I didn't tell him I'd seen Marco through the window of the hotel room later that night. He'd pulled up in his pick-up truck, leaned an arm out the window and spat onto the asphalt before driving away. The two officers spent a long time unpicking the Hotel Amancay situation. They didn't believe I'd gone all the way into town just on account of some bugs falling from the roof onto my lonely bed at the farm. They also asked me if my bed was lonely. At first I said it was; later, I hedged my response with ambiguities. Did I know if Marco had any enemies? they continued. Did he owe anybody money? I said no in all the appropriate places and spoke at length about Madame Cupin's dresses, about her habit of going out for a walk at sunset, about her walking stick that got stuck in the mud during the rainy season. I cried in all the appropriate places, but they didn't think much of my tears.

I was with Alexander, opposite the main square in Heidelberg. We were saying goodbye. The sky was limpid, unusually so, the weather barely cool. A few others had also ventured outside to refresh their lungs; inside the café, the stale smell of the long winter was still oppressive. We talked (they talked) about the weather and about how maybe tomorrow it would be properly warm. In their world this meant thirteen, perhaps fourteen degrees, should Fortune be so kind as to cast a glance at their side of the globe. The city continued on its placid course of richness and wellbeing, with its population of students and foreign servants and the well-to-do. Heartened by the prospect of pleasant weather, those gathered were making plans for a picnic. They agreed on a time and place, delegated tasks. The looks on their faces were priceless as they anticipated perspiration, feeling the sun's rays warming their necks and shoulders. I wasn't sold on the picnic idea, partly out of elegance and partly out of a longstanding inability to feel joy. But Alexander managed to convince me, and even suggested I make something to eat—not because he wanted to show me off like some kind of exotic bird but because he was genuinely and naively interested in me as a person. "Something Latin American," he specified, employing a term that, while it works in some contexts, definitely shouldn't be applied to food. The next morning, on my way to the tram stop to meet Alexander, I passed by the bakery on Hauptstraße and decided to buy something, even though I'd told myself I'd never set foot in there again. It was unusual enough that I'd stayed in the same city after quitting my job. From the street I could see the new salesgirl. She was taller than me, and able to reach the top shelves without difficulty. She sold poppy seed, she sold rye. She smiled as she handed them over, just like I had. Going inside would have meant betraying myself and sympathizing with her. I'd already been through the IKEA job, the auto-parts factory job. Going inside would have been some kind of consolation, though I'm not sure what for. The crumbs of comfort. I went inside. The salesgirl was running to and fro behind the counter. The customers beside me grumbled about the wait, about her incompetence in cutting the bread. I waited for my turn. I tried to look her in the eye, told her I sympathized with her, then left without buying anything. As I walked down the street I realized my sentence had been meaningless, something like "sympathize you" or "my sympathy." I was well accustomed to the strange animal that was my language, so this wasn't surprising to me. I met up with Alexander in Bismarck Square. He asked me for my Latin Americanisms and I told him I hadn't brought anything. He dedicated the tram trip to reeling off the extremely valid reasons (valid because they were his) why I should continue living in that den of European traditionalism, with its 500-year-old houses and its balconies dripping with flowers. He mentioned books, the peace and quiet, the university. If you found it hard to think, you could just head to the forest, or to Italy, which served as something of a last resort for all melancholy Germans. The age of traveling the world and marveling at other people's poverty was over. And yet he still felt the weight of an entire continent on his shoulder, you could see it when he walked. We got off the tram at the last stop, and he persisted with his argument as we crossed the university campus in the direction of the highway. I wondered what drove him to justify himself to me in that way. To me of all people, such a poor witness. He spoke about freedom of thought and its alleged beauty, he even spoke about social security, using words that crawled out of his mouth like tiny insects, and it was almost as though he were aware of it, because every so often he'd rub his lips to prevent them from stinging him.

My father used to sing to me at night: sleep now, little buttercup, or the dust will come and eat you up. Then he made me learn the periodic table and the chemical composition of ether. That last bit is a lie. Nobody talks about ether anymore.

Friday night in Berlin. The city seemed to promise something of a truce, as far as the weather was concerned. Julia, Kolya and I were all on our feet. Mother and son had been crying. She was in her usual stance, half-resting against the kitchen bench, and I mirrored her beside the dining table. Kolya had fallen asleep then woken up again, all tear-streaked, and his rather inauthentic weeping had provoked his mother's much more convincing version. Now the three of us were looking at one another, sizing each other up, and the kitchen seemed narrower than usual. I had a weak card up my sleeve and planned on playing it at some point. Despite Julia's insistence, Kolya refused to return to solitary confinement. He made faces and rolled his eyes, beseeching our pity. The mark on Julia's face was still visible, and the bruise had colored to a thick circle that, at a certain angle, made her look like a clown. There we were. I said to Julia that maybe we should go to the party after all, and she replied that the party had been a week ago. I wasn't intimidated by that, and soon found another party that was at least as uninteresting as the one we'd missed. Naturally Kolya didn't want to sleep, or try to sleep, in the sick neighbor's apartment across the hall. But the force of the circumstances, and the force of our arms, along with the promise that he could watch a movie even though it was already midnight, eventually convinced him. We painted our faces and changed our clothes before leaving him with the asthmatic. We took a taxi, a decision that broke several of our rules of austerity. The party I'd chosen turned out to be not very Berlin. The music was a mix of electronica and sporadic cumbia, and there wasn't a single interesting person there: no cheerful and solitary drag queens, no naked people, no bearded women. But Julia seemed pleased with the two decorative palm trees, fake or otherwise. We had a few drinks, winking at each other under the lights; it was impossible to speak. After a while she left with a guy who seemed like a "gentleman," she told me later, but it didn't work out. "It didn't work out," she told me afterward. "He wasn't good for much." And what good would he have been to me? My suitcases were still packed and stowed in the wardrobe. I saw Julia, and she made a sign at me as she walked past. I thought about going home, but I stayed; this happened several times. I thought I should wait for Julia to come past again. I stayed standing in my corner, when suddenly something caught my attention—finally, after two, three hours of sipping my drink without a single interesting thing to look at. It was surprisingly easy to recognize him, considering the number of years that had passed since I'd met him, the number of years he hadn't even crossed my mind.

I didn't want to admit that the thing befalling us was only the return of summer. I was still living in the little house, and every morning I'd walk down to the town, put on a checkered apron and a pair of gloves, and rummage for almonds or walnuts in the barrels where we kept the dried fruit and nuts. I took the customers' money and handed them change, I ate, I breathed suspiciously the unavoidable fragrance of thyme and aniseed. I'd leave in the afternoon and sometimes I'd go for a walk down the main street, looking at the dust-covered novelties in the shop windows. On that particular afternoon I walked all the way to the payphone center. I had a vague desire to call Julia, as I'd done that one time last winter, only this time I'd actually follow through with it. Another dead name,

Alexander's, somehow found its way into my head. Confused, I opened the door and bumped into somebody. It was Marco. We looked at one another with a suspicion that neither of us could fathom, but refrained from asking what each of us was doing using a telephone that wasn't the farm telephone. A mutual "good afternoon" and a nod, that was all. Inside, I hesitated over whether or not to buy a packet of colorful sweets; but I wasn't there to buy sweets, I was there to swallow the bitter pill of my love for those distant people I'd left for dead, so many years ago. The kid at the front desk offered me a booth, which I declined.

The enraged customer returns to the Heidelberg bakery and I manage to hurl a jar of jam which hits him in the shoulder, but doesn't break. The jar rolls along the floor and still doesn't break. At that moment, more than ever, I despise the Germans' world-famous quality-assurance standards.

It was five-thirty in the morning, according to the Turk's watch. He was nervous for the first time in his life, biting his moustache, exposing the stained enamel of his teeth. With considerable difficulty, I asked him what was wrong. He didn't answer me. He finished his coffee with an air of theatrical solemnity, shaking the last drops into his mouth, then dropped his empty cup onto the table that served as a barrier between us. Moments later I heard a scream, followed by a howl. Everybody in the cafeteria stood up, except the Turk. Then, with what seemed to be a great deal of effort, he rose from his seat and half-heartedly joined in the general commentary: "How strange?" "What on earth?" "What could have happened?" We walked out in single file, just like in the evacuations we'd practiced, though fire was the last thing on our minds. An accident had occurred in the store. It had been the boss's idea to construct a tower of five thousand red and white plates, in the shape of a skyward-pointing arrow. We'd all been reticent that morning when she recruited builders for her monstrosity. Only the Lithuanian had shown any interest. She was entrusted with the task, which she undertook with seeming diligence over the course of several days. On one side, a red arrow pointing toward the sky—toward the future, the boss had said—and on the other side the IKEA logo. It was a work of art. And now it had been reduced to a great monolith of rubble. The Lithuanian scrambled to uncover some item of clothing that would reveal the identity of the person buried underneath it. But she knew full well who it was. First a hand appeared, then its corresponding wrist. Someone recognized the boss's gold watch. They dug her out. They called an ambulance. One of the cult members even let out a hypocritical sob, whimpering "poor little boss" or "my poor boss" or something like that.

"In the Hotel Amancay, then?"

"In the Hotel Amancay. Without fail."

The baker stopped talking to me. He no longer called me out back to perform our tired comedy of the disappointed boss and the foolish assistant. Nor did he come stomping out to the cash register to dictate his numbers at me. It's possible the jam-jar customer filed some kind of complaint against him, but I can't be sure. The owner didn't even hint at it the day when, after all the cakes had been sold and the food that would otherwise have been thrown out had been divided among the employees, she called me into the private kingdom of her patisserie. The white-bonneted salesgirls were mopping the floors; the bakery was closed. I accepted her offer of a bite to eat, and was even allowed to try a few of the delicacies usually reserved for special occasions. I had already prepared my farewell, which was to be executed frankly and without preamble, but the coffee and sweets confused me. Hadn't she brought me here to fire me? In a nutshell, and in a totally unforeseen turn of events, the owner told me that by end of the year I'd have the right to legal work status. She'd provide me with papers and benefits, all sealed and approved. The night before, I'd gotten into a fight with the night watchman at my student hostel; I'd forfeited my room and packed and unpacked my suitcase for the third time. I had so few belongings, and still I couldn't make up my mind. I had the money for Portugal. Why Portugal? I imagined that, in Portugal, I'd be able to get a breather from the stifling sense of European self-sufficiency, and perhaps hear some beautiful lachrymose melodies. The sea would be the Atlantic: that also factored into my decision. Corsica, Greece and Turkey were still ineluctably steeped in the old waters of the Mediterranean, with all its ruins and sunken ships. I ate all the pastries the bonneted salesgirl brought me one by one, before thanking the owner and telling her yes. I had to commit to staying at the bakery for at least two years, she explained. Then she shook my hand, feigning affection. She even prepared me a special takeaway package so that I could celebrate my great victory at home that night. Maybe she didn't know about the jam-jar incident. Tonight I didn't have to do the bathrooms or the floors, she said. The bonneted girls looked at me from the corners of their eyes. Walking back to the four walls I called home, I started to knit fantasies out of all the money that awaited me: the change of work status wouldn't guarantee me a raise straight away, but eventually it would. If I saved for long enough I'd be able to move into my own apartment, or travel somewhere, like other people did when the summer vacation bell sounded—I could go somewhere and then *come back*. In bed that night, surrounded by canapés, I lay imagining and dismissing my future lives with a Napoleonic hand to my heart.

A man in a red cap opened the elevator door for me and a man in a red cap closed it on the ground floor when I got out. Stefan was waiting for me at the breakfast table, beneath a grand oriental ceiling. We drank tea prepared with water from the Nile River, and discussed the rancid breath of the camels.

We'd eaten, and now the sky turned its back on us. The fair weather held out until we took our last mouthfuls; soon after, the clouds closed in and it was as if the sun had never been there at all. Nevertheless, they tried to continue their celebratory spring picnic. They passed around suspicious-looking cold meats smeared with mysterious sauces, and opened packets of sweets, but nobody wanted to eat any more. One of the party, who apparently hadn't been informed of my origins ("Aren't you Turkish?") was busy disparaging the politics of Latin America. He'd traveled to several countries in the Americas and had confirmed for himself the backwardness of our ideas and the corruption of our institutions. He was one of those ignorant know-it-alls who manage to gatecrash every gathering. Spring billowed up in kilometer-high clouds, and we were soiled slowly by a gathering wind that worried the picnic implements. In the wake of my cultural superior's comments, a very civilized discussion unfolded on the triumphs of liberty and reason, and although a few of them revealed, like an unstitched hem, the guilt behind their Nazi past and the misdeeds of colonialism, to which Europe still owed a great deal of its wealth and progress, the group as a whole seemed terribly satisfied with themselves and with their cordial, democratic world. One in particular seemed to consider himself some kind of apostle of social progress, and spent a while trying to convince me of the wonders of European transparency and the international market. The others, even the ignorant know-it-all, made sure to partake in the usual game of without-a-doubts and but-of-courses, in an attempt to throw a cheerful veil over their criticism of the rest of the world. Except Alexander. He looked at me every now and again, fixedly, from across the sheet that served as picnic blanket and tablecloth.

Choose Heidelberg! Alexander said. Choose Berlin! Julia said.

My heart isn't even good at being bad.

Later, returning home arm in arm beneath an intermittent rain that had been the cause of much anxiety at the picnic, he told me he was ashamed of those people and swore that next time he'd throw punches at some of them. I'd heard that sentiment before, and told him I didn't need him to swear anything to me. But Alexander insisted, and despite the cold wind that had picked up he stopped and told me over and over again, his face red with earnestness, that freedom also meant misfortune, that it also meant the freedom to be unfree. He particularly liked this last bit, and repeated it again when we got home. The freedom to be unfree. I took his clothes off and pushed him into the shower. It was colder inside the shower than it was outside, and the water took a century to warm up. Afterward we got into bed and settled our quarrel with the oldest of remedies. And for a moment we felt victorious, and the magic of sex was renewed, and we were better. I looked at the German ceiling and the German windows, the bed where I lay and the table beyond. I thought that I loved all of it tremendously, as if discovering the thought for the first time. I told Alexander that I wouldn't go back to the student hostel, not even to pack my bags. He could bring my meager possessions over whenever he felt like it. I wanted to stay here, forever. Truly: I never ever wanted to leave.

I glimpsed them as soon as I stepped through the gate. They were sitting underneath the walnut tree: Marco on a tree stump, the other on a green canvas chair that folded up like an umbrella. Later on, I discovered him sitting on the same chair in the middle of a field. It must have been some kind of good-luck charm. From afar the two of them looked similar, but this impression died as I got closer, because the other one greeted me with a warmth Marco never would have shown. He even took his hat off, and folded his mouth into a strange friendly grimace that vanished as soon as he turned his face away. They spent the afternoon together, in silence. They went to look at the crops. They mounted their horses and headed out into the fields. That night they had dinner at Madame Cupin's house; through the illuminated window I saw them drinking from deep glasses of wine, engrossed in what I imagined was a very serious conversation, judging by their expressions and the shapes made by their shoulders and arms. The next day, as I pulled weeds from the few remaining peony beds, he came over to introduce himself. He shook my hand quite formally, and told me he was very sorry I hadn't been at dinner the night before.

"I'm just renting the little house next door," I said, feigning humility.

"That doesn't matter. My mother would have liked to invite you. She prepared an exquisite rabbit. Do you like rabbit?"

"I don't think so."

He left, carrying his little green canvas chair and accompanied by a farmhand and a dog. He was too well dressed for the farm and the heat. He returned covered in mud and full of enthusiasm, despite the rain. He was clutching a notebook and a flower: for me, he said. I asked him how many poems he had in his notebook and he said none, only plans and numbers, like the good architect he was. That night Marco slipped into my house without a sound, and the puerile thought occurred to me that he'd come to visit me in spite of the others, as some kind of act of defiance. But his mother and brother had gone into town, and there was nobody in the other houses or underneath the walnut tree. A few caresses was all it took to arouse in me that peculiar sadness one often feels when, despite all evidence to the contrary, one suspects that one is loved. Or half-suspects, always with an eye open, to ensure the prey doesn't escape. His brother the architect lived in Chile, he told me, and for years now he'd wanted to build a big hotel on the third and farthest plot, the eight-hectare one by the hillside. He talked about investors and made big plans, but Marco and his mother still weren't convinced. Sometimes they argued, yelling and screaming about their ancestry. After pretending to be civil for a while, I told Marco to leave, that I didn't like being his secret anymore. But he stayed, and I surrendered, until the others came back and Marco slipped out the kitchen door, acting as though he'd just been feeding the pigs.

Back in Buenos Aires, fatherless, after ten years of dragging my bones through the Old World, having acquainted myself with the Antilles and the white stone façades of Tunisia, I find myself in my brother's house, walled in by suburbia. It's a double-story house with a lot of bedrooms, and a morning silence punctured by the barking of dogs and the whirring of vacuum cleaners. The kids are at school. A woman a few years younger than my mother would be, if she were alive, is wiping the dining room furniture with an orange cloth. The lady of the house must be at the hairdresser. I have a room to myself, which is more than enough for me, but still. They said I could paint it any color I like, which is to say that my brother would pay someone to paint it for me. I could easily spend several months in that bedroom without spending a cent, without subjecting myself to the yoke of any job. It's afternoon, and one of my brother's daughters comes home. She makes several cunning attempts at winning me over, without success. Head to head at the dining table, we complete her biology homework together. The wife comes home too, and offers me a snack. Better not, I say. I go up to my room and sit at the desk where, stacked into tall deliberate piles, my brother has left a number of science books rescued from my father's house, on the assumption that they once belonged to me. I look down at them and open the window. The next-door neighbor's garden appears; I see a cat hunting something invisible to me. I decide to stay in Buenos Aires. I'm tired of this haste, this incomprehensible urgency. I probably think about Julia, about how she was always right about everything. I decide I'm tired of the life I know. I decide to change my dust jacket, change my hair. On a piece of paper I will later misplace, I scribble down some equations with several unknowns: a, b, c.

Julia was a woman with such good intentions. She claimed the only thing that mattered to her was love. If you saw her laughing, or holding Kolya, you believed every word.

That night in Berlin, at the party, I recognized Stefan among the hundreds of unfamiliar faces. I even remembered his name. He had to dig deep into his past to recall my face, and the rest of me.

"Málaga," I reminded him.

This password from the past didn't seem to work, and I had to try a thousand different memories before he understood. Finally he did, or at least he managed plausibly to pretend that he did, and we spent a long time side by side studying each other's drinks. I'd lost sight of Julia, who had disappeared with the "gentleman" and had no intention of returning. I used her as an excuse to stay in the club another hour, even though I hated it there. I didn't know what to do with Stefan. He asked me several times if we'd really met in Málaga. He was convinced he'd never been there, although apparently he'd traveled Spain extensively, as he had the rest of Europe and the entire planet. I said it had definitely been Málaga, and that he'd been traveling with a four-year-old who hunted lizards in the shrubs. He admitted that he did, in fact, have a son somewhere. Where? He was in London some of the time, Singapore the rest. A pale woman like an ear of wheat appeared behind us and stroked his back. We continued talking with difficulty under the barrage of music, growing slowly and modestly drunk. The pale woman leaned over, revealing her cleavage, to whisper something in his ear. Nevertheless, Stefan said he hadn't come with anyone, and we walked out together into the Berlin night, which is unlike any other night. He glanced at his watch, made a calculation, then extracted the latest piece of technology from his pocket and spoke to it in English, then wrote something in Chinese, greeting and farewelling people in every corner of the globe, as we walked together along this street and that street, aimlessly at first, then along the banks of the canal. Suddenly he put his device away and asked me what I was doing in Germany. To begin with I lied to him, taking thousands of pointless precautions, but then I said something true: that I'd come to Germany to look for him, first in Heilbronn and then in Heidelberg, because those were the two cities I thought I remembered him mentioning that night in Málaga, when we'd met and his son had hunted imaginary lizards in the shrubs. That, he replied, couldn't possibly be true. He'd never been to Heidelberg, except as a child, and he'd certainly never been to Heilbronn. I must have gotten confused, I said. But he was enthralled, he asked me questions as if he cared about my story. He was killing time; it must have been too early to call some other corner of the world. One by one I gave him the lies he requested of me. Why come to Germany to look for him if we'd only spent a single night together? I didn't tell him the truth: "So I wouldn't have to go home."

I wander, I wander, I wander. I dream of Bedouins and tides.

It's been raining for ten days, sometimes a little and sometimes a lot, according to meteorological laws that transcend the little patio where I sit watching the falling water, at different times and from different angles. The rain isn't threatening; we even welcomed it at first. But now the water opens channels in the earth (where the soil allows it, or fails to prevent it) to form new streams and lakes. It's a simple process, one that invites contemplation and melancholy: first the land was dry, then it was green, now it is flooded. Before there was no lake there, no pond or puddle, and now there is. It takes every ounce of my feeble willpower to avoid succumbing to the hypnotic traps of mountain life. I fetch strawberries, I feed cats, I eat raw peas off the vine, all without lapsing into a state of reverie. A man approaches; I recognize him from afar, but only barely. I know a little about his past. He wears a black beret that adorns his head like a bow. He's carrying a few extra kilos, and an awful smile that he misuses to ask me the whereabouts of Marco as I sit shelling peas into a bag. I offer him some peas. He tries one, then another, and another, spitting them out one by one. I tell him they're delicious; he disagrees. Then I tell him his animals are stranded, that if he likes I can help him move them. He studies the axe that Marco has left too blatantly in the middle of the porch. It's a good axe, he tells me, without enthusiasm or secrecy, a very good axe, I'd know, I used to work as a lumberer in El Hoyo, I'm telling you it's a good axe. Ask him if he'll sell it to me. He even leaves me his telephone number. He doesn't move the sheep, doesn't say goodbye, but before turning back he removes the beret and smooths his glorious head of hair, which doesn't look like the hair of a murderer.

"How many dead?" I ask Marco when he returns to the farm that night. "The lumberjack from El Hoyo was here."

"I don't remember," he says. "Maybe none." He directs a kick at a cat sneaking under the eaves to avoid the rain.

Our boss, or what was left of her, was removed from the store on a stretcher. Her face and uniform were still decorated with red and white porcelain shards. We didn't see her again. Rumor had it she died before she even got to the hospital. This seemed like an exaggeration, and I tried my best to deny it. I was worried the Turk would be accused of something, and by denying the facts I felt that I was somehow contributing to his salvation. But neither he nor the Lithuanian seemed worried at all. They feigned normality for a few weeks; only one or two broken plates, no mysteriously stained sheets. Through their shared conspiracy they had come to love one another. But I never saw them leaving work together, never heard them discussing a film they'd seen or a night they'd spent together. They communicated in taunts, like teenage boys or sailors. As she passed him in the store she'd say: "Working hard, huh?" or give him a little shove, or pull his hair, or swipe one of his aromatic black cigarettes. Our replacement boss turned out to be much friendlier than her predecessor. Now and then, if she was feeling particularly inspired, she even managed to call some of us by our names. The odd innocuous accident still occurred, and occasionally we'd catch wind of some complaint from the sales staff regarding our arrangement of the merchandise. Many mornings, on my way to work, I resolved to join forces with the Turk and the Lithuanian, to praise their sabotage with my primordial tongue and convince them of my potential worth. I tried, and I could not. For some time now the Turk had stopped offering me his cigarettes, and he no longer invited me to sit at the conspirators' table. The two of them seemed to be approaching the apex of some secret project when the Lithuanian stopped turning up regularly to work. Sometimes she'd arrive with a black eye, poorly masked with makeup. He found a way to comfort her during the breaks, in the bathroom or the women's change rooms. They stopped joking around, stopped taunting one another. The Turk's happiness faded slowly, like a dying light. One day, we simply didn't see her anymore. She disappeared suddenly, just as the boss had, only this time there was no ambulance, no stretcher, no procession. And the Turk mourned her in secret; this I know, although he never spoke her name again.

"Are you sure I have to go?"

"Yes."

"You're absolutely sure?"

"I'm always sure."

"Please," I begged. I wasn't used to begging. I'd survived my first winter on the mountain. I'd been living in the little house for over half a year, and was now working for the health-food shop in town, selling flour and almonds. I had a wad of savings rolled up inside a tin can: money I'd received from my brothers, mostly, money that rained down from the black sky of their distant compassion. But as far as Marco knew, I had no money. Where will I go? I asked him. I said I'd do anything if he'd just let me stay.

With no wife and next to no sex life, my father went back to physics as soon as he turned fifty. He knew the subject well, because he'd thrown his heart and soul into it in his youth, before he met my mother and abandoned "All that stuff," by which he meant science, in order to enter the rodent wheel of real life: earn money, have children, earn more money. But at fifty he suddenly found himself without a wife, and the old song of family and material comfort began to lose its charm. Lumbering, like an old dog, he went back to the wisdom of his first love. He didn't believe in rest, not even in the last months of his life, when he couldn't get out of bed to use the bathroom or look at himself in the mirror. He always had his pockets filled with ifs and buts. If someone said "sky" he'd pull out the old "atmosphere" trick; if someone said "rest" he'd bring up the perpetual movement of the stars and atoms. He died triumphantly skeptical, or so I was told, in the same bed he'd been confined to for months. He died with his arms full of clocks. He'd had every clock in the house brought to his room and scattered across his bed. My brothers didn't understand why, and neither did my sisters-in-law. It was just one of his eccentricities, one of them said when I returned to Buenos Aires. It was his way of saying goodbye to time, I said.

We struggled, but it was a false struggle. I fell to the ground, or let myself fall, and Marco threw himself on top of me. I would have liked to explain to him the complex interweavings of nature before we made love, but he didn't care for stories— not even our story—and he abhorred explanations. From my very first night in the little house on the Del Monje farm I'd been weighing up the possibilities of this happening. Would he or would he not come to visit me one night? Would he or would he not warn me beforehand: "I'm coming to visit you tonight"? These questions braided themselves into huge spider webs that I, weak human specimen that I was, all protein, tissue and brain, was incapable of ripping apart. But we'd been pursuing each other for a while now. He and his mother rarely set foot inside my house. The cats came in, though (they weren't allowed in the other houses), as did the dogs, and occasionally the tame sheep who always expected my leftover pickings. These visits only occurred when their owners weren't looking: Madame Cupin certainly would not have approved, and if Marco had found out he would have stormed inside to kick them out. He is calmer out in the fields: he speaks to me mildly about strawberries, or the recent frost. He tells me about the corn and the apple trees, and I glimpse great mysteries behind the simplest of weeds. One day I asked him if he had a woman in town, someone he visited when he went out in the truck to sell lamb or buy provisions. He didn't answer me. I understood that I'd said too much. I tried again another time, also outside, beneath the thick nose of the mountain: "Do you have a woman?" No, he says, and crouches down to uproot an encroaching weed. Later on it is night, or close to it. In spring, the sun sets much later. I go out onto the patio to turn off the tap that is watering the peonies. The heat is harsh for this time of year; it's only October. I go out wearing very little, since I've just taken a shower and it's warm and the patio is deserted. I walk a few meters to turn off the tap, which has already flooded one of the flowerbeds. I turn back toward my little house and see him standing there, in the middle of the patio—he's probably been watching me this whole time. I understand that he is wearing more clothes than I am, and that this gives him some kind of insurmountable advantage. We measure each other up, neither of us lowering our gaze. It's a long minute of nothing. I explain that I just took a shower and forgot I'd left the tap running. "Of course," he says. I tell him that's why I came outside. Difficult as it is, I turn my back on him. From the doorway I bid him goodnight. He doesn't answer me, doesn't move a centimeter, nor does he take his eyes off me. I could have hidden inside my house. But I didn't. I waited for him. He approaches me and I let him. He touches my cheek and I offer it to him. One of us has just won a prize, but I'm not sure who.

That cold and probably damp night, we grew bored of walking along the canal. We hailed a taxi, and got out after a few blocks. Julia's house was empty. We didn't loiter in any of the rooms, nor did we bother to turn on the heating (which, according to custom, was always turned off when nobody was at home to enjoy its benefits). We didn't pause in the kitchen to make a cup of tea. He removed his shoes. How many years had it been—eight? nine?—since we'd met in that seaside city of Málaga? We talked for a while, unnecessarily, about his well-paid cosmopolitan job, his travels, the incomprehensibility of languages and the wonders of English.

"I prefer Hong Kong to London," he said, unprompted.

I particularly liked the way he closed his eyes, the way he crowned every phrase with a sarcastic little laugh that, with time, I would come to mistrust. And even though he wasn't interested, he asked me about my life in Germany during those forgotten years. I invented a few stories: that I'd lived on the coast of the North Sea, that I'd married a man who managed fishing boats. I'm sure he didn't believe a word of it. It was cold so I got into bed with my clothes on, which complicated matters later on. Stefan took a long time to follow me under the covers, because he received a call from the other side of the world, closing some deal at a cost of untold jobs. Such things excited him so much that I—that is, the woman I was back then—barely registered in comparison. After the phone call he told me to get out of bed and take my clothes off, slowly. I refused. But he wasn't the kind of man to be deterred by obstacles; for him, my resistance was the whole point. He undressed himself instead, and as he did I understood why I'd been attracted to him all those years ago, why I'd used him as an excuse to leave Málaga. Once he was in bed with me I thwarted every one of his movements: if he wanted my mouth I gave him my hand, if he wanted my hair I gave him kisses. We persecuted one another for a long time upon those four square meters of mattress. But something was left unresolved, because the following night we made plans to meet again in his hotel, where we replayed the same scene, acted out the same comedy. This went on for days. Soon he had to leave—he had heads to tear off, heads on the other side of the globe. Did I want to come with him? In Berlin there was Julia and Kolya under the yellow light in the kitchen, where the three of us had eaten together for years. In Berlin I had a family, I had a whole box of good intentions, you might say, that we'd been filling up together for the future. I'd fallen in love with them both, mother and son. And yet, what is one to do, when faced with oneself? Cut and run, if that's what you know best.

A constant westerly wind blew across the lake from the Pacific, via the mountains. We'd left late, under Madame Cupin's disapproving gaze, which had fallen apart at the last minute once all her ploys to prevent us leaving together had failed. She'd insisted on taking the canoe across with us, so as to personally deliver Monsieur Cupin's immaculate pile of books (which we were donating in his name) to Rural School Number Fourteen, which was only accessible by water, or by horseback if you took a long and winding detour. Her reluctance had pushed our departure past midday. We'd left her standing under the eaves, posed bitterly against her walking stick. We'd also had to pass through the town before continuing on to the lake, to deliver three animals to the lumberjack from El Hoyo. The gravel roads offered up a plethora of potholes and other obstacles, which posed little challenge to Marco's truck. Marco had refused to tie up the last sheep, which we were to exchange for some wood from a man who lived a little way up the mountain, and the poor thing knocked around violently in the back. It was delivered on time, albeit a little jelly-legged.

We carried our payment back to the truck and continued on to the lake shore, where another, bespectacled man was waiting for us with the hired canoe. Each of Marco's interactions with the locals entailed the exchange of new and not-so-new gossip. The canoe man insisted he'd felt an earthquake two nights ago. And that the lumberjack from El Hoyo, a known outlaw, had been stealing his logs when he wasn't home. We'd already discussed the earthquake with the man at the service station, who claimed it hadn't happened, and the man from El Hoyo, who assured us his brother had been thrown from his chair by the force of it. We set out to cross the lake. They told us there was too much wind, they advised us not to go. But Marco said we'd have a tailwind on the way back, and that we'd easily make it home before nightfall. I'd heard about the water in the lake, but I never anticipated it could be so transparent, even in spite of its depth: over three hundred meters, I was told.

"It's cold," Marco warned as I plunged my arm in.

It was freezing. I managed to feign composure, told him it could be worse. From the very first night we'd spent together he'd made a point of never letting his gaze linger on me any longer than it would on any other living creature, never uttering any especially meaningful words to me. Our bundle of French books was balanced on the floor of the canoe; there were two treatises on mechanics and several adventure novels. Three hundred meters below us there waved the green peaks of a long-lost forest. This should have been cause for long dull exclamations of admiration, but Marco paddled on in silence, and I followed suit, suffering as I did from the defect of happiness. We arrived late and exhausted at the other side of the lake, our arms burning. We ascended the steep slope of the

shore, pricking ourselves on sweet briar rose and grabbing at
broom bushes to pull ourselves up. It was all in vain. The school
was closed, the doors padlocked shut. There was nothing for
us to do but leave the books sitting on a pile of bricks next to
the entrance, where they would not be protected from the dew
and rain. Then we made our way back to the shore. The canoe
slipped back into the water with barely a push. Night was beginning to fall in the forest—we could smell it—and the wind
had changed. It blew enormous and glad against our faces.

Back then I wanted to hunt lions, I wanted to commiserate
with the poor. Alexander didn't understand this. He observed
me from the bed with tired eyes. What good were his social
sciences if they failed to convince even a single solitary woman
to stay. He had no more reasons. So many ideas about Europe and human dignity, and now he had nothing left. He was
naked, twice naked. Meanwhile, I repacked the suitcases I'd
emptied one month earlier. He kept on trying, in fits and starts:
we could fix things if we traveled together, if we started a family, if I found a better job. Why had I married him? That very
night he'd speak to his friend, the physicist, and finally secure
me the job in the laboratory. He'd call a friend who worked in
a pharmacy a few hours from Heidelberg. His ideas died one
by one, like so many poisoned moths. I refused everything, and
even though I wasn't finished packing I closed my suitcases as
best I could, which was badly, and kicked and dragged them
down the stairs. They clattered scandalously all the way down.
Where was my victory? Alexander followed me, boarded the
tram with me, helped me with my things when we got to the
train station. In the ticket queue we let people in front of us,

not wanting to advance. This game went on for a while, ten, fifteen minutes, as we fought with our tears and our ineluctable goodbyes. When I finally bought my ticket to Berlin, it felt like the greatest accomplishment of my life. Alexander said he didn't want to say goodbye, and left suddenly. But later I saw him on the platform, where I was sitting on my bags waiting to board. He removed his scarf, tied it around my neck. We hugged and I promised him so many things: that I'd come back, that I loved him, all of them lies.

Why all that trouble if in the end I'd broken the laws of physics anyway? Why, I wondered, if after so many years of pilgrimage I'd finally found my place? Marco, sitting with the wood and the axe before him, scratched at the earth with his dirty boot. We spoke politely, the sheep bleating beside us.

"You'll have to leave in two months, three at the most."

"For any particular reason?"

"We're restructuring."

"And you want me to leave?"

"No, I don't."

The one who wanted me to leave was Madame Cupin. Later that afternoon she came to my house to bring me some clothes that, according to her, she hadn't used in years and were now too big for her: Parisian handkerchiefs, one green and one red; an alpaca wool pullover; a number of other luxury items that were of little use to me. I should consider myself privileged, she said, to receive such precious gifts. Not everyone was deserving of such gifts.

I can smell night descending. He disappears behind me, into the forest, in search of branches and something to eat. I rest my head once more against the cold earth. And the planet has stopped spinning. And I've stopped with it.

"I don't want to leave!" I cried as he retreated.

"Any love interests?"

None that I was aware of, I say.

"Well, there was Lali," the other policeman intervenes.

They exchange a wink.

It can't be true, I think from afar. The cow's blood falls in a thick stream upon the grass. The sky darkens and it's afternoon. I thought it couldn't be true because they'd talked about it so many times, but nothing had ever happened. I've always had an exceptional capacity for skepticism. They always said today, or tomorrow, or the next day, but the day never came. And now today was the day, and the cow pumped blood until it collapsed on its side. Marco made a second cut, in case the first hadn't finished the job, but it had, there was nothing left but flesh. They'd grown sick of waiting for the butcher, so Marco had recruited one of the neighbors' sons who sometimes hired himself out as a farmhand. A drafthorse dragged the cow's body to a tree, where they strung it up with chains and pulleys. It was a meticulous process: first they opened up the chest and carefully separated the meat, then they removed the legs. A slender boy of around ten, who had gathered around with a few others, stuck his fingers elatedly into the animal's eyes, its stomach, its intestines, without rupturing any of the tissue. They skinned the body with care, so as not to damage the leather, and emptied its guts. The cow's three hundred and fifty kilograms barely swayed in the breeze. Marco made a sign at me and I rinsed out the bucket where he'd washed the bloody knife, which wasn't an easy job. Then we sat down on a tree stump a few meters away and discussed the various methods for killing cows, sheep and goats, and as he explained this to me he rubbed his hands with a cloth stained overly red. An acidic odor of fermenting grass issued from the carcass, and I wondered if I actually liked that man, if I would actually let him touch me with those bloody hands of his. Spring had not yet arrived. I worked all day in town and gazed at the mountain on my way home, predicting a life for myself; for real this time, this time forever. There was not a trace of emotional blackmail. I hear him chopping wood and I go outside, even though it's dark. I offer him something warm to drink, because my heart betrays me and drives me to do the stupidest things; it convinces me to love a man who ignores me and spends his afternoons slaughtering lambs and gutting sheep. Marco pauses, and for a moment the axe is suspended in midair. Then he lets it fall and tells me no, he doesn't want anything to drink.

I'm indefatigably happy. Even adversity brings me joy. The cold, the snow, the empty chair across from me at the dinner table, where I now sit down to eat.

At heart I'm no good, even for acts of justice. Everyone had left: the owner had gone to fetch reinforcements from among her family members, the baker was out collecting sacks of flour from the supplier. We were all overwhelmed by the hustle and bustle of the festive season, and the customers swarmed in search of fat and sugar like the eager flies they were. The cash register opened and closed before me. Notes came and went. There was enough money in there to fund the long holiday I'd promised myself, once the festive season was over. On the first of January I'd finally be a legal employee, and to ring in the new year I was planning to take some time off. "Where will you go?" the owner asked me. And then, with a hopeful tone, since she was a mother after all, she added: "Back home?" "Definitely," I replied. Back then my lies were reluctant and unpolished, and I dragged them from my mouth with sorrow. Looking down at the cash register, I thought the right thing to do would be to set aside the money owed to me and hide it in my pocket. An impulse to flee trembled in one side of my head, just above the temple. I counted and separated the notes as a bluish-faced man selected a dessert for his family's Christmas dinner. I threw in a little extra to cover my Christmas bonus. The flies buzzed impatiently on the other side of the counter. It would have been an act of enormous purity, leaving like that, with the cash in my pocket and the bakery packed with people. But perfection isn't meant for us all. I wasted my time with Blue Face and with the man behind him, who wanted a poppy-seed loaf, and then with the man behind him, whom the snow had marked with a black stain on each shoulder. Even with my feet burning with pain, and the money burning a hole in pocket, I kept smiling obediently until the baker returned, crossing the room with long strides. Later on he complained to me about the number of customers *expecting*—that was the word he used—bread and cakes. This was how he managed to be both rich and miserable at once. All seemed lost, but when he retreated to the depths of the bakery I saw him slap the door with his palm, as he always did. This final repetition was all it took. I removed my apron and crossed to the other side of the counter. They say the flesh is weak, but the conscience is weaker. I went back to the cash register and returned the money. A customer asked me what I was doing. I told him the only thing I knew: "I'm leaving."

Another customer tried to stop me, without success.

My jacket was still hanging from the coat stand, inside the bakery. I walked along the white street, wetting my shoes and admiring the lights. What was new about this? Nothing. I was cold and I walked, despising the bags of presents and the Christmas greetings people lavished on one another. I went into a café and spent all the coins I had left. I didn't want to go back to the bedroom I knew by heart, the one I'd already tried to leave more than once. I walked down to the bridge and, rather theatrically, tossed my residency card and the ticket I'd just bought to Portugal into the river. The river was frozen, so they didn't sink. I looked at them for a while, thinking that tomorrow, if resolve failed me, I could always try and rescue them. But that night resolve didn't fail me; that night was the most triumphant of all, because I had nothing in my pockets, not even my own name, and nothing in my heart.

I think about it, and I think about it, and I don't think I can do it. I've lost my flair for the art of flight I practiced so diligently in Africa, in Asia and Europe. I pace between the kitchen and the bedroom, inside the little house, which is dark. I have to go and I don't want to go. Outside there is a very clean moon, a sincere-faced moon, which turns the patio and the sheep and the walnut tree into distant relics of an abandoned city.

It's better if his mother doesn't see us, he tells me. He takes the truck on a long detour, parking a little way past the farm. He crosses the field alone, to find me a change of clothes. Our rough night at the lake, under the open sky, shows on our faces. I need to change my trousers before heading to work.

He comes back to the truck and I notice the trousers he's brought are of little use to me, but I don't say anything.

"She might have seen us already," he says once we're in town, sitting across the road from Mágica y Natural, where I work.

"I don't understand. Why can't she see us?"

"Because it's not good."

I didn't find out any more that day. I sold pepper and semo-lina flour and everything else within my reach, trying not to write out too many receipts, just as I'd been taught. I was so obedient sometimes. But as soon as I had a free moment my mind started to spin with probabilities and questions. The local drunk came in asking for food and we offered him water crackers and a little bit of water, which he refused. Madame Cupin had been disturbed, or disarmed, or enraged. She seemed, or she was, kind toward me; but then there was the walking stick stuck in the mud, and the pearls and the axe, and the Viennese handkerchiefs, and all the rest. My mind spun around and around, for hours and days. How I wished I could dismount from the carousel of my life.

Julia was crying and Kolya was crying. When we left the the-ater I asked them: what's the point in shedding tears over the misfortunes of strangers, especially when those strangers are just puppets, fictitious creatures made of cloth? Kolya couldn't answer, and Julia forgave my lack of tact. I took them home and prepared what must have been a kind of celebratory dinner, because we'd just decided to move to a larger apartment. Julia had already begun the process of indebting herself to a bank, and I would contribute by paying the bills every month. She'd made lots and lots of calculations, and I'd made several promises, and Kolya ran around brandishing a doll and howling with happiness. But promises are made of an indecipherable substance, one whose atomic and molecular structures are extremely fickle and unstable. Over dinner we discussed the puppet show we'd seen that afternoon. We tried to explain to Kolya the way puppets were manipulated. We tried and tried. He didn't understand. From that moment alarm bells began to sound, distant at first, but sure enough they heralded something: the setting in motion of my departure mechanism.

"Do you think he might be slow?" I asked Julia when we got up from the table.

She shook her head and tried to ignore me. I flamboyantly threw what remained of our banquet into the garbage, even though I'd been told to keep some leftovers for the next morning. Later she asked me to put Kolya to bed, and to buy cigarettes if I went out, but I did neither; I shut myself in my room. My life's work was stashed away in the wardrobe: an immaculate pile of bags and suitcases. I went back out and explained to Julia that I was sick of looking at her day in and day out.

"I'm sick to death of looking at your face," I told her.

Julia was intelligent and honest. She had mothered and grandmothered a lot of pain over the years. But it was late, and she'd already exhausted her reserves of psychic science and geniality. She said all those funny words Germans use to insult one another: stupid cow, female goat, among other zoologisms. I felt elated, and laughed aloud to myself as I walked in and out of the cube that, until a few minutes ago, had been my bedroom. How ridiculous the doors and windows seemed to me now. How absurd the feet on the furniture! I stood on a chair and tried to cut the cord off the ceiling lamp, but even on tiptoes I couldn't manage it. Simply turning off the light seemed inadequate.

"You're not even going to say goodbye to Kolya?" Julia said as I dragged my suitcases down the hall. The taxi had arrived and was waiting for me a few meters down the road. I opened the front door with difficulty, holding my handbag between my teeth. Julia went to enormous lengths to avoid helping me, rubbing her hands together in the cold. She had finally ditched the last of her beauty. Suddenly she looked very young. She tried not to look at me, or love me. She said the same thing my father had said to me ten years earlier.

"You're going to regret this."

That afternoon I disembarked from the plane, as I had from so many other planes he'd booked and paid for. Stefan walked half a meter ahead of me, as he always did, dragging his latest-generation suitcase behind him. At the customs desk I botched a couple of words in English. I ignored the clamorous propositions of the taxi drivers. But this wasn't Tunisia or China. I told Stefan I was going to the bathroom, and hid inside the café on the first floor of Ezeiza airport. I found a table right at the back. I knew it would be a long time before he thought to look for me. A while later I got up and scraped together a few yen, which I exchanged for pesos and used to call one of my brothers. He answered. He even pretended he was happy to hear my voice.

I'd spent the night in town. In the morning I walked back to the house, up the dirt path. It was strangely silent; there was nobody around. Marco's truck was parked under the walnut tree, instead of in its usual spot. This seemed like a bad sign. One of the wheels was crushing the budding peonies. There didn't seem to be any sign of the insect infestation Marco had warned me about. I approached the house and realized that the front door was open. I looked inside. I saw one of Marco's arms, one of the arms I'd adored for so long, and it wasn't the same as before. I saw an arm on the ground painted dark red, the same color as the walls. The bloodstains crawled toward the ceiling like an army of ants. But it wasn't insects, as Marco had promised it would be.

"There are going to be showers tonight," he'd said.

"How do you know?"

"Because it's the season for it. And it's warm."

I didn't ask him what kind of insects they were. I didn't even stop to wonder whether they were coleoptera or dipterans. All Marco told me was that they rained down from the ceiling once a year, and that they liked to get into the bed sheets and disrupt the sleep of whomever they encountered there. I no longer sought terminology or referred to things by their Latin names. I'd gone to El Bolsón as instructed, and sat waiting beside the window of the Hotel Amancay. I'd simply taken his word for it, delirious with a dry, intoxicating happiness, trusting that he would come.

And now? Seeing that arm, I understood how an entire world can unravel in an instant. I didn't dare go through the door. I ran to Madame Cupin's house to tell her something terrible had happened, to ask her to help me. But her house was empty. A cat smiled down at me from the eaves. I crossed the patio and tried Marco's house. Also empty; that much was to be expected. I didn't have any telephone numbers I could call for help. Even as I ran breathlessly down to the cabins in the hollow, I knew there was no need to rush, that nothing depended on my actions now. I spoke as best I could to the person I found there: one of the bearded brothers. The other brother went out to notify the firefighters and one of his neighbors, who was a doctor. We walked back to the farm and I wasn't allowed to approach the house for a long time. The morning seemed like an arduous, starless night. Finally a very round man with extremely bright eyes appeared, and confirmed the worst. Marco was dead, as was his mother, who had been found in my bedroom. Was this even possible? It was much more than possible.

The white walls of Greece—or was it Tunisia?—gleamed in the midday sun. Stefan called to me from the bed. I went to the bedroom and let myself fall against the sheets. His cologne, which was expensive and more exotic than most, lingered on the pillow, and I didn't want to feel it touching my cheek. He'd unfolded every single device, every screen and microphone, so as not to miss anything that was going on in the world, and also so that nobody would forget about him. He took great pains to remind everybody of his presence at every opportunity, as though he were in fear of dying, or already dead. He had a thousand hands and spoke a thousand languages.

"Do you like the hotel?"

I liked being far away, that much I knew. With a slight caress he invited me to engage in some kind of negotiation, and I accepted. For a while we imported and exported the humors of the body, until we were interrupted by yet another phone call. I went back out to the balcony. The sea was the same stain it had always been. After the phone call Stefan came over to stroke my back. Apparently he felt this was an opportune moment to destroy my innocence (as he put it). I didn't want to listen to him, but I did. His sarcasm was like the music of a vile instrument burning in my ears. He talked about how they manufactured teacups in Cambodia, which sold for a pittance in Australia and Singapore. About the Australians who bought them in the supermarket, and then donate twenty cents to a UNICEF campaign at the register. Didn't I think this was magnificent? Wasn't our world a work of art?

One of his devices sounded again from the bedroom. I heard him speaking in English, precisely on the topic of a shipment of Cambodian teacups stranded at a port in Sydney. Guys like Stefan are so bad at making up examples. I stood before the great blue stain of the ocean, thinking about how yesterday had been my birthday: thirty-three years old.

It's cold, despite the carpet covering the floor and half of the walls. I'm incognito in Buenos Aires, no one is pursuing me. It's petty victories like this that I delight in. What is this apartment? An empty square of bricks on the top floor of a building in the suburb of Once. The sky I'm lucky enough to have chanced upon is yellow and filled with smudges of humidity. I look out at the grimy uneven rooftops of the city where I was born. My father was wrong: there is such a thing as repose, and it exists beneath an old tree that spits walnuts in March.

"That's quite an accent!" said doña Carmen of La Mancha. We set out from the hotel with the humble aim of buying bread and jamón. The heat was exhausting, and I was hesitant to breathe it in.

I light the water heater, take off my dirty clothes and step into the shower. I'm wasting the tank water. I've lived in the little house for some time now, and I don't want to leave. Outside, it is snowing. I get out of the shower and dry myself carefully. I perch on the edge of the bathtub to put on some clean tights. They are neither old nor new. As though creeping up from my feet, happiness fills my throat. It's such a great privilege to get out of the shower and put on clean stockings. I was standing, but now I have to sit back down because the tears are falling all the way to my knees.

"Do I really have to leave?"

"Just for tonight. The bugs will be swarming tonight and you won't be able to sleep."

It's true that it was very warm that night. I spent what remained of the afternoon cleaning the vegetable baskets. I sold some carrots to one of the neighbors and watched Marco coming and going, with logs and without logs, delivering and returning sheep, his truck battering up and down the dirty trail. He told me to pick some tomatoes, even though they were still green. He loaded the truck with two bags of potatoes and then unloaded them. He looked harried, he cut wood even though we already had more than enough for that time of year. I decided not to ask him the destination of the inedible tomatoes, nor why he'd left the axe in the middle of the garden again. He was strictly economical; he never did anything that wasn't necessary. And he was careful. He hated working in vain. Only with me did he squander resources, never knowing how or why. I touched his arm, although we weren't accustomed to displaying affection out in the open—being visible meant being careless.

"Maybe you could stay with me in town tonight."

"Better not."

"Please? We could go out for a walk. Or look for some music."

"Not tonight, I think."

Was this hesitation? I couldn't help asking:

"Do you have other plans? Or is it because of Madame Cupin?"

Marco didn't answer me. He picked up the axe and decapitated several thick logs, which he then split into strips. He worked swiftly, with the precision of an artist, but he was as merciless as a butcher. I despised his terseness now more than ever, I was offended by it. It felt like he was wielding it against me. I told myself: "I don't love him. I never want to see him again."

I went down to the road on foot. It was one of those misty winter mornings in the mountains, when even the trees are almost invisible. I was up very early, and there were still several hours before I had to be at work. I stuck out my thumb, but no cars stopped for me. I walked with a certain apprehension along the side of the road; it was the sort of morning when drivers might veer off the road, always braking too late, or just in time to fracture someone's arm or a leg. Why was I so worried about the integrity of my physical person, if I'd made such an effort over the years to throw myself off precipices, to submerge myself, to lose myself at borders? Because that morning, very early, with the mountain still shrouded in darkness, I'd come to a realization: my father had lied to me. The little house lost in the mountains, cold in the winter and oppressive in the summer, with its patio and its walnut tree, was irrefutable proof of this. For the first time in my life I could sit and recline without a shred of skepticism, trusting completely in the resilience of chairs and beds. Anyone could come along with their science now and refute the evidence of my nights and days. I had become a magnificent animal: soft, compact, whole. When I arrived in town I had to ask them to open the payphone center early, because it wasn't yet nine o'clock. I was there to revive the dead. My heart pounded in double time. I dialed a long number and waited on the crackling line. Nobody home? But then a miniscule voice like a little bell greeted me in German. So Kolya was alive, and he was home alone. It seemed forced and pointless to try and explain to him who I was.

"Your mama's not home? I wanted to tell her. And thank her. Because love exists and the place exists."

There was an immense silence—poor Kolya, there on the other side of the phone.

"Mama went across to the neighbor. The neighbor wasn't good."

Perhaps it was better this way, not saying anything to her.

"I'm going to school."

"Yes, Kolya. That's good."

"In school I'm learning one, two and three."

Was it time yet? Alexander had put on a shirt and suit, and I barely recognized him. I pretended I'd forgotten all about it. He didn't believe me, we laughed. I also had to wear a special suit, a white one that I'd bought the day before. His parents were waiting for us at the door of the Heidelberg city hall, where the civil ceremony would take place. She dark and tall, he a little heavy and just as towering. We held hands. They smiled, said they were surprised. Due to a momentary lapse of vigilance on my part, the man stroked my head. I didn't deserve any of their blessings. Inside, a few of Alexander's friends were scattered throughout the large hall. Several of them were bunched in the corner, making fun of a royal portrait; others just looked bored. Someone had brought bouquets of carnations. *Dianthus caryophyllus*. I spent the entire ceremony running through the names of herbaceous plant families in my head, while the justice of the peace lectured us on the boons of love and married life. To his credit, he did manage to convert us to the faith of matrimony for about a month. Alexander didn't let go of my hand the whole time. I loved him as he kissed me and I loved him as we walked out into the street. But thoughts of silicon and lanceolate leaves wouldn't leave me in peace; my head was one big beaker of swirling gasses and vapors.

I sold a rye loaf; I placed a second loaf in my bag.

Madame Cupin was waiting for us with her tall wine glasses. But the candles weren't meant to be romantic; not unusually, the power had gone out across the entire mountain. We arrived together, as though we'd left from the same house and traveled a long way to get there. Despite her walking stick and her rheumatism she wouldn't let us help her with the plates or the salad or the meat, all of which she kindly brought out to us, the strands of her pearl necklace swinging as she bent over the table.

"How are you both?" she began, once all the food had been served, as though she hadn't been watching me from her garden an hour earlier. She'd seen Marco even more recently, since he was the one who'd delivered the meat that now lay soaking in its own juices atop the table. We answered individually, each mentioning some small detail from our daily lives. But she didn't seem satisfied. She wanted to know if it was true that we'd gone into town together the night before. It had been a coincidence, Marco explained. This was a battle he could never win. He denied me as many times as he could during that dinner, more than seventy times seven, if I can put it that way. Marco knew nothing about me, and Madame Cupin was triumphant in her skepticism, and my heart didn't want to be offended, it was quiet, fascinated by the glimmering of her pearls.

"And you don't get lonely in that house all by yourself?" the lady wanted to know. "Not even at night?"

She begged us to eat dessert, and dished out large portions. This time she used the plates as an excuse to whisk me into the kitchen. She served me a whisky and assured me that Marco had fallen asleep in the armchair waiting for us.

"Do you love him?" she asked once she had me cornered. I didn't answer, and this only bolstered her victory. Later on, I dared to say that I was happy in the little house they had rented to me, that I felt grateful, that I hoped I wouldn't have to leave.

"You are a charming young lady," Madame Cupin lied to me at the end of the night, and in my innocence I believed that everything would be all right.

I sold four packets of myrrh incense and a necklace of thick beads. A while later, someone threw a coin into my coffee cup.

I arrived at Retiro as the sun was setting. It was the first time I'd retraced my steps in many years. Since leaving Buenos Aires at twenty-three I'd managed to plot a simple and erratic circle across the globe, never treading on my own footprints. I even stayed at the same traveler's hotel on Avenida Libertador, because again there were no buses leaving that night and I had to wait until the next morning.

But in the hotel, unlike the first time, I didn't pretend to be anyone except the person I was. I gave my name and the address of an apartment in Once, where I still live. The twenty-hour bus ride was grueling; I was afraid and excited. Why go back now, after everything that had happened? I craved repetition, down to the finest detail: I wanted to get off the bus, walk to the fire station, cross the road, continue past the cabins, then walk up to the little house on the patio, even if it had already been knocked down. I disembarked in El Bolsón, at the ticket kiosk that serves as a bus station, and sat down on a wooden bench to let a woolly stray dog lick my hands. Someone had left a newspaper on the ground. I picked it up. In the crime section I saw an article on the trial of Marco and Madame Cupin's alleged murderers, which had kept half of Patagonia abuzz for several months. Meanwhile, I'd locked myself inside an apartment in Buenos Aires, looking out at the buildings and their terraced rooftops, trying not to think about snow or mountains. That night I slept in El Bolsón, badly. My head spilled the same thoughts over and over again from its dark depths, like a relentless fountain. Did I know the handcuffed men in the photo? Of course I did. One of them was the lumberjack from El Hoyo, the one we'd sold sheep to several times, the one I'd sold bread to at the health-food shop and fruit to at the farm. They claimed the double murder had been a hit, organized in advance and confirmed that fateful morning with a phone call. They said the voice on the telephone could have belonged to a man or a woman. The details of their testimonies were given further down, but I didn't read them; I scrunched up the page, and kicked the dog as I got up.

How many people did I use as a shield? As many as I needed.

On the tram back to Heidelberg I came across a Turkish moustache I knew well. Not once had we bumped into one another on our respective journeys home from IKEA, so I felt there must be a reason for this coincidence. Had he followed me? To find out, I decided to follow him. He got off after my usual stop and walked into an Italian pizzeria, where he ordered something to eat. I waited outside, watching as a woman served him a plate and immediately sat down at his table. Their farewell was affectionate. Then he walked a few blocks and got on a bus. There were enough passengers that I was able to avoid detection. But I didn't notice him get off the bus until it was too late. I got off at the stop after his. I walked three blocks through the clean and empty suburbs of Heidelberg, with eyes in the windows of every house. The two of them were there together, at the entrance of a building. The house couldn't have belonged to either of them, judging by the abandon with which they kissed. I was envious of their sly little situation, and stood there in the middle of the street long enough for them to notice me. We studied each other for a moment. Apparently it was neither good nor bad that I'd seen them. I turned and left. They must have closed the door she'd been holding open with her foot; they must have gone up to their secret hideout in search of pleasure, with no higher motive than to love one other completely. I retraced my path, envying them every step of the way. I boarded the tram and got off at Bismarck Square. I saw two drunk youths kicking an empty beer can around. I decided I would report them the next day at IKEA. The Lithu-anian had arranged a pile of plates that had fallen on our boss, she'd stained sheets with red marker, she'd broken glasses in secret. Other accusations occurred to me as I made my way up to my room. I was ecstatic in my misery. I planned to go to bed early, as I always did, because I had to get up in the middle of the night to arrive at work on time. But at eight o'clock I was still pacing back and forth between the fridge and the dining table; by ten o'clock I realized that I would have liked to kiss the Turk on the mouth, to smoke his cigarettes, that I would have preferred the danger he symbolized to every one of my good alibis. I never went back to IKEA, not to report them or for any other reason.

• • •

What could be more miserable than believing in God? And yet, when I saw the blood-spattered arm I began to pray that God existed, even though there was nobody there to witness it.

Marco was never one to doubt. But this time Marco doubts: he runs and catches me. Then he withdraws and pushes me away, to the other side of the fence. This confuses me. I look at him, trying to guess what his decision will be. His life is at stake, and he doesn't know it. But finally I do as he says and go into town. I take a stroll, walk past the payphone center, and end up asking for a room in the Hotel Amancay. I lock myself inside, looking out. "It's just for tonight," I tell myself. Later I recognize his truck parked outside the hotel. He's come to spend the night with me, just as I asked. Why don't I open the window and call out to him? His face is as somber as a tombstone. Before leaving, he sticks his head out the truck window.

Months had passed. I was in a Coto supermarket in Once, choosing a can of peas that I could pay for and consume, although none of them were as good as the ones on the farm, and they were all expensive. This brand or that one? I was entangled in this meticulous decision when I thought of him. The strap of my purse slipped from my shoulder and slid down my arm to the ground. I picked it up slowly, as if I'd suddenly fallen very ill. I abandoned my trolley, my umbrella, the bag of clothes I'd planned to take to the laundromat. I left the supermarket and thought that the cars were making an enormous racket along Avenida Rivadavia. I sat down in the plaza. Shortly afterward, a man came along and sat down beside me.

He spent a long time with the pigeons. Like me, everyone had their eyes on him. All the faces in the world passed by.

But it would be an act of vandalism to say that he did it for me. Anyone who's ever lived near El Hoyo knows the story of the lumberjack who killed the old empanada lady. Anyone might have sold him sheep in exchange for wood, or served him one afternoon if he came to buy strawberries. It couldn't have been the brother, who'd come from Chile to claim his inheritance and build his big hotel. It couldn't have been the French relative Madame Cupin spoke of as though he were a wealthy pirate, thirsty for a hectare of forest to spend his retirement on. That was why I'd seen him in the payphone center that day, when we'd bumped into each other at the door and he'd tried to ignore me, too slow to hide one of the green silk handkerchiefs his mother had brought back from Paris. That was why he'd auctioned off half of his best animals at such a low price, why the axe had turned into just another garden tool, loitering there on the patio under the walnut tree, like a cat. He must have hired the hit men himself. It's possible that the French relative didn't even exist. Marco hires the lumberjack from El Hoyo because he can't do it himself. But he makes sure the man doesn't know who's paying him; he calls from a payphone in town, he must use the green handkerchief to disguise his voice. The crime itself is simple. The murder weapon is waiting at the front door, underneath the walnut tree, as if someone has forgotten to bring it inside. The forgotten axe is one of Marco's pretenses, surely. But that night of the insects they arrive earlier than planned, or they arrive too late. And it's not one man, but two. For the first time in his life, Marco doubted. He's been in doubt for a few hours now. He thinks about heading into town with me, just like I asked him to, but then he thinks better of it, perhaps to avoid rousing suspicion. In any case, he decides to stay home. But he doubts, he's on the verge of regret. A little while later he drives into town, but he doesn't even get out of his truck. He parks for a moment outside the Hotel Amancay, spits out the window, then drives off. There's no way to stop the wheel he's set in motion. If he were to stay, he would give himself away. He returns to the farm and looks for his mother, who for some reason isn't in her house; she's in the little house in the middle, which is mine.

Sitting there in the plaza, I think about the crime. I sit for hours. Or are they minutes? It's afternoon and evening and morning and afternoon.

He's been planning it for a long time, perhaps since the day he first tells me I'll have to move out of the little house. Then he argues with Madame Cupin, and succeeds in winning me a little more time, because by now he knows what I'm looking for there on the mountain, and he's looking for the same thing. They're inside my house, they hear noises outside. He knows who it is, but he's surprised to see two people in the living room. Because he only hired one: the lumberjack from El Hoyo. Now that he regrets his decision, the fact that there are two of them is a huge disadvantage. Killing one's mother is not the same as killing a horse or a dog—this is what he must think, in his regret. When he finds her, a little before the others arrive, he says: "What are you doing here?" She is emptying drawers in my bedroom. They hear noises, and he goes into the living room. He doesn't have his shotgun with him. He uses a chair, a stick, a pot plant heavy with earth, but nothing can defend him against the axe that he himself left under the tree for the murderer to collect. Now it's two against one. Madame Cupin must be hiding in the bedroom. It's a slow massacre, there in the living room, where only a few hours earlier Marco and I had promised each other something akin to the future. Now he is fighting tooth and nail and arm, and they cut him open. They bring him down and then they take care of Madame Cupin.

I embraced doña Carmen in the town of Almagro, under the midday sun of La Mancha. I promised I would see her again, knowing that I never would.

I looked at Alexander, standing there on the platform, and made a gesture of love to him, but I didn't love him.

I kissed Julia's hand from inside the taxi as she, trembling in the Berlin cold, fought back tears.

I never saw any of them again. I never spoke to any of them again, never replied to any of their messages. I put an end to them all, I didn't leave a trace, didn't feel a trace of remorse. These are all my crimes: all my goodbyes.

It's turned out to be a perfect evening—it's snowing, I'm rugged up in sheepskin, and there is a white path stretching before me. I've just left my job, thrown my personal documents into the sea, and walked out of my room. I've left a suitcase in Hamburg Square, accumulating damp. I hope someone steals it, out of pity. With every step I bury a sentence, a name, until I've buried them all. I am twenty-six years old and I am brand new. Now that I have nothing, I think everything belongs to me.

He goes in search of his mother, who is rummaging through the drawers in my bedroom, and he forgets to pick up the axe he left under the walnut tree. Before the first blow is struck he manages to tell his assailant which stone the money was hidden under—the hit man's payment, which he must have already collected. If not, he wouldn't be there. It's an attempt to stall him. But, faced with the axe, Marco doesn't remember how many times he changed his voice and gave his telephoned instructions: go to the Del Monje farm and kill whoever's there. The cash is under a stone after the first rise in the mountain, at the third curve in the path, at the foot of the burned pine. It doesn't work, the second blow falls. He is big and strong, and this sparks the others' rage. They silence him with blows and then they take care of Madame Cupin. I saw him from the window of the hotel that summer night, when the insects were meant to rain down. He parked his truck and spat out the window. This was always his plan: to doubt, right to the very last; to make as if he'd conceded at the last minute to sleep with me in the Hotel Amancay. If we'd actually planned it, if it had been a real date like the ones other men and women make when they love each other and their love is out in the open, he wouldn't have had contingency on his side. He would have planned to be out of the house, and this would have seemed suspicious. This was his plan—this, or something like this. But that night he has doubts, real doubts and fake doubts. This is his undoing.

My home, after all this time? My home is the atomic number for silicon, it is the properties of butane gas. In them I relax and stretch out my legs as if in a great armchair.

He sticks his face out the car window one last time, a face that isn't his, a face that is already gone, and spits onto the ground. I see him, I see. Why don't I beg him to come up? Why don't I save him? He spits and spits, and I sit in silence.

Much later I saw the baker in a Heidelberg street, far from the bakery and the white aprons we used to use. He was a different man: not better, not worse. He recognized me from a distance, and just as we were about to pass one another he crossed to the other side of the street.

My third trip to El Bolsón was a slow one. The asphalt was full of traps. I was tired of all the questions I'd already answered; I didn't want to hear them anymore. Along the way I looked at the green countryside, the dry pampa, the Neuquén meseta. I awoke and we were approaching the cordillera, although there were still several hours to wait before I'd set foot on the mountain again. This would be the second time since his death. I didn't want to believe any of it: that the houses had been demolished, that construction had started on the big upmarket hotel Marco's brother had designed. In town, everyone had decided that the project had no future; this wasn't the kind of place anybody got rich from, it was hard enough here just to survive. I walked unhurriedly up the road, all the way to the fire station, where they waved at me with brief enthusiasm and informed me that the hit men were on remand at the prison in Esquel. Since it hadn't been a robbery, there was a lot of speculation about who had hired them. They had nothing on Marco's brother. They had nothing on the neighbor, despite his bitter argument with Marco over a water channel so many years earlier, and despite the rumors surrounding the fire that had devoured half of his fruit trees. The firefighters were drinking tepid yerba mate; they offered me a sip, which I accepted. It wasn't the fire season, it had been raining for weeks. One of the firefighters was betting on Marco's brother, said the evidence was right there in front of our faces: *he* had been the one to inherit the farm, and he'd started construction immediately on that pointless hotel, which of course was bound to fail. The other, who was born in the area and knew a lot about revenge, was convinced that the neighbor from up the hill had been the one to order the hit. Marco had shot two of his dogs and one of his horses—the blond one—after the water-channel argument. Of the fire there were only whispered suspicions. But there was motive in spades. Madame Cupin had not been the principal target—her only fault lay in being the heir's mother, or perhaps she'd simply been in the wrong place at the wrong time. Which wrong place? My bedroom.

"Thank God you weren't there that night."

"You dodged it by a whisker."

"It must have been the brother, don't you think?"

"No," I said, "I think it was me."

They found this entertaining. The one on the left gave me a friendly slap on the arm, which I allowed. At those latitudes women were considered too foolish to be guilty of anything. We spoke about the bad weather and the coming summer, the behavior of the tourists, who were awful, and the most recent car crash on the road to El Bolsón.

"You should believe me," I said as I took my leave.

They assured me that when I came back in a few months everything would be better. That we'd know more about the crime, that the mountain would be the same as ever. I should rest easy.

"Julia," I whisper. I walk on tiptoes to her bedroom, which is dark despite the daylight outside; it smells of sour flowers, one of her bad perfumes I've somehow learned to love. She is a white shadow against the bed. Her head is crowned with handkerchiefs that she dabs intermittently into a bowl of ice. She offers me her hand. She doesn't usually speak during her migraine episodes, but this time she does. She tells me useless things, ridiculous things, and asks me to do the same. We spill our hearts out as usual, although this time in very quiet voices and in darkness and with great angst, even more than usual, because this isn't doing her any good and it does nothing to mollify me or rouse in me the tingling of perpetual love.

"That," she concludes somewhat faintly, "is because they didn't have enough proof of love."

She's telling me about two people who didn't manage to make a happy ending of their love story—we spoke about such things all the time. This afternoon, though, with Berlin cloaked in haze outside the shuttered windows, Julia made an effort to explain their failure to me. Proof of love: that thing one lover demands of another; that thing that makes no sense; that capricious, that cursed thing. She gets worked up, propped there in the middle of her bed, beneath her turban of cloth and ice, and a spiral of spit escapes from her mouth.

"People demand it without explanation: I want you to

come tomorrow, I don't want you to come, and so on. A train trip, a resignation, it all works the same way," she rhapsodizes, squeezing my hand in hers, trusting that she has convinced me of something.

Four years have passed since I moved into this apartment in the suburb of Once, where I look out at the rooftops of Buenos Aires. If I stand on my tiptoes and stretch my neck out, I can see the roof of a house that used to be mine, my father's, my brothers', a long time ago. I have a table, two chairs, a blanket and a bathtub. That's all I need.

"I'd do anything to stay."
"That's not true," said Julia. "You'd do anything to leave."

In the plaza in Once a man approaches, dragging one of his legs behind him. He is a beggar. He sits beside me, ignoring me, and enters into a long and one-sided conversation with the pigeons. I slip a hand into my bag and pull out Madame Cupin's pearl necklace. I hand it to him immediately, without an explanation, except to say that the necklace is his now. He wants to know if the pearls are real. I say they're not and expel a final tear, which seems to hover in the air for a moment, except it doesn't.

I started down the dirt track and heard somebody following me. It was Marco. He put a hand on my neck and, trembling a little, since he'd jogged to catch me, bent to give me a long kiss. Why this goodbye, if we'd be seeing one another again so soon?

One hundred meters earlier he'd promised to spend the night with me in town. I'd asked him to. I'd dared to tell him that, this time, I really meant it.

"In the Hotel Amancay?" I said, stroking his face. If he didn't come, I would miss him.

"Tonight in the Hotel Amancay. Without fail."

MARIANA DIMÓPULOS was born in Buenos Aires in 1973. A writer and a translator, she is the author of three novels, as well as short stories and nonfiction, including a critical study on the work of Walter Benjamin. She teaches at the University of Buenos Aires, and contributes to the cultural supplements of Argentine newspapers. *All My Goodbyes* is her first novel to appear in English.

ALICE WHITMORE is a Melbourne-based writer and literary translator. Her previous translation from the Spanish was Guillermo Fadanelli's novella *See You At Breakfast?* She lectures in literary studies and translation at Monash University.

Transit Books is a nonprofit publisher of international and American literature, based in Oakland, California. Founded in 2015, Transit Books is committed to the discovery and promotion of enduring works that carry readers across borders and communities. Visit us online to learn more about our forthcoming titles, events, and opportunities to support our mission.

TRANSITBOOKS.ORG